JIBBY The Cat

BOOKS BY FELIX SALTEN

BAMBI

PERRI

BAMBI'S CHILDREN

A FOREST WORLD

GOOD COMRADES

JIBBY The Cat

JIBBY
the *Cat*

By FELIX SALTEN

Illustrated by Fritz Kredel

JULIAN MESSNER, INC.

NEW YORK

PUBLISHED BY JULIAN MESSNER, INC.
8 WEST 40TH STREET, NEW YORK

PRINTED IN THE UNITED STATES OF AMERICA

CONTENTS

JIBBY The Cat

CHAPTER I

ESCAPE

THE SLEEPING KITTENS made a soft furry heap against the striped body of the mother cat. Then the pile of gray and black heaved, and a white nose and mouth nuzzled to the top. There were three kittens. One was solid black; one was gray without any markings; and the third, which was waking up, had a snowy chest and white markings on her face and paws. The rest of her was going to look like her mother—dark gray with black tiger stripes running round her body and legs. She opened her baby-blue eyes, startling in their circles of black fur, and stood up.

Carrying her tail high and straight like the mast on a sailing vessel, she ventured forth into the wide barn. She took dainty, mincing steps over the loose straw. Her hind legs were weak and she staggered as she made a sharp turn to skirt the pair of upturned sawtrees in her path. Her pale eyes stared straight ahead seeing nothing but the light where it streamed into the old barn, and big dark shapes of things and creatures. A faint breeze crossing the barn floor from the open door ruffled the thin white fur on her chest, and she sneezed—a convulsive jerk of the little head and a short wheeze. Awkwardly she changed direction again and headed back toward her mother where it was warm.

The barn was full of sounds. In their stalls across the barn the horses stamped and pawed the floor. The cows made a steady rustle—swishing their tails, munching hay, and blowing out their breath. But the young explorer paid no attention. She had learned that great dark shapes made these sounds and that they meant her no harm. There were other shapes—upright and two-legged—that also made noises far above the kitten's head. They too had not harmed her; and she feared them no more than, in her natural innocence, she feared anything at all. Her whole life thus far—she was three weeks old, going on four— had been spent in the old stone barn, and she had found nothing to be afraid of.

She had journeyed everywhere—even into the stalls, where she had backed away in caution from the hoofs of the huge shapes that were in them. She still treated such things with respect, though long since she had realized their owners knew when she was near by. She had staggered up and down the expanse of open floor littered with straw and hay, and sniffed the piles of idle farm implements beside the great door that swung wide to admit a team and wagon. She knew how to scamper away nimbly at the jangle of harness and rumble of heavy wheels. On her wanderings of late she had met her black brother or her gray sister. Mostly she ignored them, but once in a while she lifted a white paw and pushed against one or the other in a signal of familiarity.

She moved on an invisible axis connected with the mother cat in the corner and she always found her way back to the warmth and food under her mother's body.

[3]

Nearing this haven, she was halted by noises coming from the barn door. She stopped and turned to look. Two tall upright forms, making the strange rumble she had heard before, were coming into her corner. The kitten turned again toward her mother and gave an odd sideways leap that landed her on top of her sleeping brother and sister. She snuggled down between them, eyes closing with delight, pink mouth opening suddenly in a great yawn.

Sleep was already washing over her when she felt a clasp around her neck. It was not her mother, the grip of whose jaws or paws would not have awakened her. One of the upright shapes had taken hold of her. The kitten made no outcry, for it had happened before; she had been swooped up high and held close to them while they made their funny noises right in her face. Always after a little while they put her carefully down again.

Now everything was different. Instead of laying her down where she belonged, the creature that held her turned and carried her away from the mother cat's bed in the home corner and out into the very bright light.

Squinting her eyes against the painful brightness, the kitten began to struggle, squirming and wriggling

[4]

in the big firm grasp. Something cuffed her on the nose. Once, far behind her now, she heard her mother's voice raised in terrible anger. Close by, her black brother and her gray sister set up a thin meowing. The other man—for that is what they were —had one of them in each fist. But the white-breasted tiger kitten could not cry; her mouth opened and stayed open in a meow of fear that never came.

Below her the ground moved too fast. What she saw made her dizzy—a vast openness in place of the sheltered dusk of the home barn. The grasp on her neck shifted to her middle, which made it hard for her to get her breath. The hand that held her swung back and forth as the man strode along. Ground and sky moved and swayed, making her dizzier than ever. Beneath her it changed color from the brown bare earth of the barnyard to the lush green of high thick grass. Again she tried to get free, but her spread claws scratched the empty air.

Then they came to a stop.

All was silence except for two distant splashes. The black kitten and the gray kitten had stopped meowing, but their sister did not notice. She had forgotten them completely.

"This one is a beauty," said the man that held her.

[5]

"No," boomed the other. "One cat is enough to feed and pamper on a small farm. All three must be drowned." It was only a thunder of noise to the helpless kitten, but her panic mounted.

Now the ground moved so fast that she could not see. The painful grasp on her body was gone, but there was nothing under her. A rush of air took her breath away. She was falling.

Splash!

The kitten hit the cold wetness of the river and her heart pounded with terror and pain. All four legs in their white ankle-high boots beat feebly one after the other against this last and greatest catastrophe; but the strong current rolled her along like a ball of black, gray, and white fluff. She closed her eyes weakly.

School was out for the day, and the boy Peter went whistling along the narrow pasture path above the noisy rushing stream that marked one boundary of his father's acres. When Peter whistled it was not out of timidity but because, like any boy or bird, he felt like whistling. Besides, though he was going a little out of his way, he was still on his father's land. Farmer Julius owned all the acres on this side of the river. Across on the far side lay four smaller farms, their fields running down to the water's edge.

The brawling stream widened and grew quiet, turned swampy, and then lost itself in a broad lake. The single beat of a cowbell traveled through the still air. Peter stopped whistling and broke into a run. He ran the last half of the way to his little beach out of fairness to his father, who expected him home to do the before-supper chores. Also, if he did not linger too long, Peter would not have to explain what he had been doing.

A brisk onshore breeze was blowing, and lake-sized waves lapped the hidden little semicircle of gravelly beach. Peter sat on his heels and watched the shape of the dainty waves that ran curling and light-crested up the beach to break in a series of gentle slaps on the shore. The late sun got in his eyes; and, looking away upstream, he saw out of the corner of his eye something white floating on the lake. He stood up and faced the sun, shading his eyes to keep the bobbing object in sight. Peter's private beach was a great satisfaction to him. Something always happened there.

Was it a piece of cloth that he could salvage for

his tree-tent? It was too big for an open milkweed pod; the season, moreover, was too early. He waited for it to drift nearer, for the breeze and the waves were driving it gently toward him.

Two more waves, and Peter's heart gave a jump. He ran a few steps forward to the wet edge of the shore and looked down at his heavy shoes. Then he waded a few paces into the shallow water, stooped, and picked up the inert little grayish ball.

"A kitten!" he said aloud in a shocked voice.

He raised his eyes and looked across the lake toward the farms on the other side.

"A kitten!" he said again wonderingly to himself, lifting it up and cradling the thin, bedraggled body in the crook of his elbow.

The kitten lay still, breathing weakly, aware of nothing.

"Are you still alive?" the boy urged gently.

The kitten heard him, sensed friendliness, and tried to meow. Nothing came of this effort; her mouth did not even open.

The boy laid her out on a flat sun-warmed stone and, squatting on his heels so that his body acted as a windbreak, he watched her intently for any signs of life. Lying dully on her side, pink skin show-

[8]

ing between wet hanks of assorted white, gray, and black fur, the kitten was such a sorry sight that Peter loved her. He began to hate the people who had tried to kill her.

Peter was ten, and he knew people drowned kittens—his father for one. His eyes blurred with tears, and a difficult new pride in his brusk father came over him. His father might be hard on kittens, but he did not throw them into the river with careless cruelty.

The kitten whined softly. The afternoon sun, hot and strong, was drying her fur. Her head moved a little, jerked to a stop, and then moved again. The tiny mouth opened very slowly; and the minute whine turned into a recognizable meow, though it was barely more than a helpless complaint.

"Bravo!" Peter cheered. "Good for you!"

When the kitten began to cough, Peter held her upside down, head dangling, and gently rubbed her belly and chest. River water spurted out of the little pink mouth onto the gravel at the stone's edge. The boy smoothed and dried her fur a little, using a blue bandana from the pocket of his jeans. Delicately he picked up the limp body, holding it against his chest, and started back along the lake path toward the turn-off for the farm. He glanced at the sun: it was not too late. What luck that it had happened so fast!

As for the kitten, ground and sky were moving fast again, and she shut her eyes against them. Little by little she grew aware of the gentleness with which she was being held. Warmth poured into her from the sun and from the boy's hands and body. She hastened to express her feelings. The note of complaint was gone from her voice. The meow sank lower, turning rhythmic and mellow.

Peter's kitten was unmistakably purring; and, if it was nine parts diplomacy, the boy did not mind. He laughed out loud and walked faster.

From the turning it was exactly half a mile home, and on the way Peter wondered how his father would receive his new friend. They had always kept a cat on the farm, not because his father liked them but because a cat held the field mice at bay. The last cat had disappeared about a month ago, and Farmer Julius had made no effort to replace her.

"There's time," he had told Peter.

The boy wasn't fooled. His father was hoping they wouldn't need another cat. When mice turned up in the barn again and forced him to get another, he was going to be angry about mice and cats alike. Peter smoothed the kitten's fur—but not too hard— and planned his campaign like a general going into a battle.

They came in sight of the farm buildings. The footpath joined the river road that ran along the gentle rise of land back from the stream. The skilful farmer who had been Julius' father had built his great stone and timber barn on the road, his house nestling behind it and off to one side like an afterthought. House and barn had their backs to each other—a highly useful arrangement for man and beast that neverthless left the front of Peter's house unused and curiously blank-looking.

Facing on the road before you came to Julius' barn, there was a small white house with a low-hanging green roof. It belonged to Victor the schoolmaster. The schoolmaster figured in Peter's plan. But Peter did not want to take the main road past Victor's front yard and the barn beyond. For Peter's father was expecting him in the barn by now. Instead Peter turned off into a little side lane that ran behind the schoolmaster's cottage and then on past his mother's kitchen door.

The schoolmaster might have been out in the front

yard with his wife and dog, but Peter was in luck: Victor was cutting the grass in the back yard. The boy slowed his pace so that he came opposite the man just as he finished a row at the bottom of the garden. The mower stopped its clatter; Peter scuffed a pebble, and Victor looked up.

"Hello, Peter," he called, smiling. "What have you got there?"

The privet hedge was between them. The schoolmaster was a tall young man with unruly black hair and dark, friendly eyes. Reversing the lawnmower and trailing it behind him, he came down to the hedge and peered over.

"About three weeks old," he pronounced—an expert opinion, considering the fact that the creature had just lost several days' growth. "Someone give you a kitten, Peter?"

Peter told him about fishing the kitten, almost dead, out of the river and Victor's eyes darkened.

"I don't think I could drown a kitten. Could you?" Victor said.

"No. No, sir, I couldn't."

"Taking her home?" The schoolmaster's tone was grave, but the smile came back into his eyes. "What will your father say?"

Peter thought it over, looking down at the kitten. Then he took a deep breath and spoke very fast.

"Would you come with me—could you, now?" he burst out. "And ask my father to let me keep her? As my own, I mean. Not just to catch mice."

Victor glanced up the lane. Two hundred yards away through the trees he could see Julius' house and the dark gray stone and weathered red siding of the huge barn. Beyond the buildings stretched Julius' corn fields. The rolling land back toward the river Julius used largely for pasture, with an experimental stand of cane in the rich bottom land by the river. Victor had lived here all his life—his father had been the schoolmaster before him—and he knew every square foot of the big farm in one corner of which his house had been tucked like a picture cut out of a storybook. Moreover, he had known Julius when the gap of ten years between their ages had seemed far wider than now. He could sympathize with Julius' ten-year-old son.

Gravely he looked back at Peter, much as one boy looks at another while they go over a matter of vast importance to them both.

"You can best settle that with your father, Peter,"

he said. "You know I only make him angry when we get on the subject of animals."

"But you know how I feel!" the boy exclaimed.

"Yes, it's important for you to have a pet." Victor nodded. "But you alone can fight for it. Honestly, you have a better chance that way."

Peter stared at him somberly. However, Victor, who knew that a moral truth is apt to sound like preaching, was relieved to detect no signs of doubt on the boy's face.

"Let me know what happens," the teacher added.

Peter nodded his head. He wasn't ready to consider a possible line of retreat; and Victor was content not to offer the hospitality of his cottage until the need arose.

"Good evening, sir," Peter said in a small voice and, glancing at the salt-and-pepper bundle silent and half asleep in his arms, he started down the road toward the next step in his campaign.

He clambered over the gate that closed off the pasture lane from the barnyard. His mother was in the kitchen where he had hoped to find her. It was important that she should see the kitten before his father did. She was at the window, setting pies out to cool on the wide sill. The hems of the red-dotted

Swiss curtains fluttered above the smoking pastry. *Canned cherry,* Peter guessed. He started talking before he was halfway up the stoop.

"Look, Mother!" he cried. "Look what I fished out of the river." The screen door banged behind him. "She was almost dead, I can tell you. She swallowed a lot of water, and it was a long time before she came alive. The people across the river did it, I guess. May I keep her, Mother? For mine, I mean."

His mother—small, square-shouldered, and strong looking in a full-skirted dark blue dress and embroidered black apron—smiled at him and the kitten before she crossed toward the stove again.

"Of course," she said, stooping to take the last pie and a small pan of cinnamon rolls from the oven— the leftover scraps of dough had made five rolls this time. Peter stood so close that the kitten's nose twitched at the heat and the new rich smells. "But you must ask your father."

Peter's face fell and he said nothing.

"You must. You know it, Peter." She looked squarely at her son over the pans she held in her hands, and then moved toward the east window that faced the orchard—the boy at her heels. They heard the father's step on the wooden stoop, and Peter whirled and faced the door as his mother moved on across the room.

Farmer Julius, a sturdy man of medium height, came in slowly, rubbing his hands together as if to work the tiredness out of them. His large brown eyes were ringed with fine wrinkles, and his skin was burned a deep brown. The red on his cheeks had a high polish. He halted just inside the door, looking at Peter and then at the kitten and saying nothing.

The boy waited a little longer. But when the explosion did not come, he knew he had to speak. The silence was the same as an order.

"I'd like to keep her, Father."

"I don't approve of pets, Peter; they're useless."

"But"—Peter took a deep breath—"they threw her in the river. Let me keep her as a pet."

"No." Julius glanced at his wife and shook his head. "If she stays, she must work. The mice are in the barn again."

"All right, Father." The words were out before Peter knew it. He moved a hand to the kitten's head as if to protect her, and opened his lips to add: *But she's mine.*

[16]

He thought suddenly of the ground he had already gained for his kitten and said nothing after all.

His mother came over to him and tickled the kitten under the chin.

"Take her out to the barn before you go for the cows," she said, tucking a cinnamon roll in his free hand. "Lay her against Lady beside the two puppies."

"Mother!" Peter protested, stuffing the sticky roll in his pocket without thinking. "They're dogs!"

"Son, this kitten is too young to eat real food. She ought to be fed by her mother for yet a while, I should think."

"But—"

"Put her against Lady's nipple. If she drinks, well and good."

"What if she doesn't?"

"Then we'll see, Peter." The words were firm, but a little smile flickered on her lips and around her eyes. The last of his worry left him. "Now you better step lively, or it will be suppertime before you and I get the milking done."

Peter's kitten snuggled forward between the two puppy dogs, reached for the maternal breast, and drank greedily, her eyes closing with delight. Lady,

[17]

the queenly shepherd dog, lifted her head and looked over her shoulder. Twice she snuffed the newcomer: and then out came her big warm tongue, almost hiding from sight the sudden addition to her family, and she began to wipe out the dampness that remained in the kitten's coat.

CHAPTER II

MIDNIGHT, THE BULL

THERE, MIDNIGHT," said the farmer, coming into the barn and stopping at the big stall next to the corncrib. Warmth crept into Julius' gruff voice. Midnight the bull was the pride of his farm. "Come now. Time to take your walk. A little exercise will do us both good."

It was mid-afternoon, the best part of the day for the sturdy farmer. The big barn was silent and empty at this hour. The cows still roamed the lakeside pasture, and Julius had unhitched the team of blacks from the plow and left them grazing in the grass at the edge of the apple orchard. Away in the back of the barn the shepherd dog, with her family of puppies and the kitten she had adopted the night before, snoozed peacefully in her corner.

Midnight snorted and stamped in his roomy box stall. He had the legendary look of the black Angus breed: the curly poll and massive square body. Julius kept his shiny black hide curried like a show animal's. A brass ring through his glistening snub nose restrained his immense strength. Every breath he drew sounded like a snort of fury. Nevertheless Midnight was a gentle bull.

Patting him gently on the flank and breast, the farmer loosened the rope running from the nose ring to a slat of the corncrib. Midnight whirled around without touching the man and stalked toward the open barn doors.

Julius followed the bull out of the stable. Catching up with him at the bottom of the barnyard, he rested a hand on the stately animal's thick neck; and together man and beast took the river road to the upper-pasture gate.

They struck across the field to the far edge, turned, and side by side like comrades walked up and down the field along the river bank. The stream sounded under the bank, the man talked steadily, and the bull rocked his broad skull in voiceless response. His ears flicked a comment now and then, and his square jowls worked all the time.

A meadowlark in the grass raised a paean of thanks from the fields to the sun.

Julius glanced at the sky.

"Well, Midnight," he said. "The hour is up. We must go home now."

Obediently the black colossus wheeled about, and they headed back across the field. The return trip was made in silence until they came to the stretch of road that ran past the teacher's cottage. A few yards away, Julius took up his gentle, running address to the bull. But Midnight was not restive.

They swung around the barn to the back, where Midnight drank at the spring-fed watering trough. He would have drunk more, but at a light touch from Julius he lifted his dripping tongue from the water. He covered the short distance to the back barn door ahead of his master and stood waiting.

Cut in the rear wall of Julius' barn was a matching pair of big doors. Like the main entrance facing the road, they too could be swung open if Julius wanted to drive his team and wagon straight through the

barn and out the far side. Except at harvest it was
closed and only the top half of the Dutch door, set
into the right-hand panel, stood open.

Behind the door—it opened on the cows' side of the
barn—was Lady's corner. Peter was crouching there.

"Grow, grow, grow," he was whispering.

Julius and the bull halted behind the boy and
watched Lady, her two puppies, and the tiger kitten.

"She's a good mother," Julius remarked.

Peter turned his head and looked up at his father.

"Do you think the kitten will grow all right?" he
asked.

"Well, a cat is always a risk," Julius replied, his
steady hand on Midnight's neck. "You never know
about cats. I don't hold with the people who say
they want to return to the jungle. Cats love idleness
and want to be cared for. Yet the finest and fattest
show a bad streak, and I think it comes from not
doing any work. The good animals, like the good
men, are the ones that work. The ones that idle and
play all the time spoil on you. But let's hope for the
best. You ought to find a name for the creature."

"A name!" Peter's face broke into a smile. His
father thought the little cat would live to grow up.
"I'll think about it, Father."

"Do that, Peter," Julius said, giving Midnight a slap on the shoulder and starting up the barn aisle after him. "Thinking is not idling: it's a form of work."

Back in his stall, Midnight stood calmly while Julius tied him up again. Fresh straw covered the floor. The box stall had been raked out and cleaned while they were gone. Julius kept his voice low as he spoke to the bull.

"Now, what do you think of that, Midnight?" he said. "The boy got home from school early today." Cleaning the eight stalls in the barn was a part of Peter's chores on Saturdays only. "Well, well," he went on, circling around the animal and taking down a currycomb and brush from the wide ledge he had built on top of the left stall wall. Stepping out into the aisle, he beat the two utensils together to knock out the white dust from the currycomb. He came back along Midnight's right flank. The bull's shoulder rippled with pleasure at his touch.

"Ready for a good rub-down?" Julius asked.

The daily grooming of Midnight was a special ritual in four parts. Using a long downward motion of the comb in his right hand, closely followed by a sweep of the brush in his right, Julius first dusted and cleaned every inch of the bull's hide. To do the legs and underbelly, the farmer sat on one of the milking stools from across the barn.

Next came the polishing—short, careful strokes that laid each hair straight in its place. Midnight's coat gleamed like black satin. For the bull's face and head, Julius switched to a special half-sized curry-comb on a sturdy handle. Here a short, upward stroke with a roll of the wrist at the end preserved the curl that marked the bull's Aberdeen-Angus breeding. This curly poll gave the bull's face the incongruously sweet look of a wooly lamb.

Finally Julius drew a double band of ruffled curry-comb stripes across the satiny coat—back of Midnight's massive shoulders and straight down both flanks from spine to belly.

Farmer Julius enjoyed his task, but he was also a highly practical man. He had set Midnight's stud fee high. Yet no farmer, stranger or friend, had ever questioned his price. Night or day a neighbor could drop in and find the bull perfectly groomed. And the canny Julius never talked price until the caller was face to face with Midnight in all his splendor.

Halfway through the grooming, when he changed

brushes, Julius heard Peter enter the open horse stall next door with the manure rake.

"Boots," he was saying in a solemn tone followed by a judicial pause. "Tiger," he intoned. "Hilda. Nora. Jane. Gertrude, Gertie." Peter sighed. "Guinevere," he said to the polished handles of the wheelbarrow standing in the open wagonway before the horse stall. The wheelbarrow was full, and Peter trundled it out through the doors and around the far side of the barn to the manure pile over at the edge of the corn field. He brought back a load of fresh straw from the stack in the middle of the barnyard.

"Mary," he pronounced. This was his mother's name and he discarded it as soon as it was spoken. "Black-eyed Susan. Susie." The boy's voice trailed off toward Lady's corner.

Giving the combs a last knock and his friend the bull a parting pat, Julius started for the spring, a drinking pail in each hand. At the swinging Dutch door he paused a moment behind Peter, who was again bending over Lady and her family.

"Susie," the boy called softly. The kitten made no response. He tried again. "Tabby, tabs," he coaxed.

Coming back from the trough with water sloshing from the buckets, Julius heard Peter's voice raised in exasperation. He was stringing together words and pieces of words in a jumble of nonsense.

"Tabbykit — jagabog — abbanonnysurbamdadly-roo." He took a deep breath.

"You've got it," said his father from behind him. "That's a good name. It doesn't make sense, but neither do cats. Gibberish and that creature fit each other."

Peter reached out and took the kitten up in his hand, holding her soft fur against his cheek.

"Jibby," he whispered. "My Jibby."

The kitten was quiet for a moment. Then she stretched her neck in the direction of Lady and the puppies, and spread all four legs. The boy put her gently down on the floor. The ceremony of naming Jibby was over.

The even days stretched into weeks. The mighty creatures came and went, the life of the barn flowed about her, and Jibby grew and changed. Harness jangled, and the cows lowed. Midnight snorted; and the horses, Flora and Sara, pounded the plank floor with their hoofs and whinnied. The calf's stall across the aisle from Lady's corner—it was boxed in like Midnight's with the same kind of low swing-door, but far smaller—remained empty. Julius curried his bull.

Home from school, Peter climbed the perpendicular wall-ladder to the great haymow overhead and pitched hay down the manger-chutes under the eaves to the eight stalls below. Then Peter went to fetch the herd. The five cows filed into the barn, their udders so full of milk that drops spilled out as they walked. Peter and his mother did the milking. Dusk and a milky steaminess enveloped the barn, and Julius brought in the team.

Soon Jibby was far ahead of her foster brothers. The puppies were still wobbling clumsily when Jibby began dancing, sure footed and full of grace, around Lady's patient head.

She toured the barn by herself. The first time she ran into Midnight's stall, she halted a foot or two from the great hind hoofs and backed slowly out under the swing-door. There she stood listening and smelling to get her bearings.

Next day she practiced climbing the oat bin all the way down the line from the bull's stall. She scrambled up the wall of the unused little stall and walked along the narrow ledge. She played in the stall and leaped delicately to the manger. Then one morning, treading the manger edge, she made her way the whole length of the stable, through the two horses' stalls and up on the wide ledge of Midnight's roomy quarters.

Curling up beside the currycombs, she looked down on the bull. Midnight gave no sign, but he knew she was there. Jibby rose, arched her back, and went back the way she had come.

One afternoon she was waiting up there when Julius and Midnight came back from the field by the river. Julius saw her when he reached for the currycomb, but he did not chase her away. Jibby kept her perch all through the long ritual.

Peter learned of this new trick on Saturday. The boy, who had not been allowed inside the bull's stall until this year—and then only to bring Midnight his measure of oats at the close of the grooming—was very proud of his kitten.

Next, Jibby discovered the barnyard and learned how to take a drink out of the tiny spillway from the water trough. Then she discovered the house, and after that she left Lady for Mrs. Julius' kitchen.

It was Monday, and Jibby romped in the grass under the billowing lines of wash hung out in the side yard. Just as Mrs. Julius was carrying a basket of folded clothes into the kitchen Jibby darted past the long skirts and into the house before the screen door slammed shut. She ran straight to the wood box and curled up along a length of peeled cedar bough.

Mrs. Julius gave her clear laugh and hunted in the cupboard. From an upper shelf she took down a heavy flat cereal bowl—it had been baby Peter's—and poured a shallow helping of milk into it. She placed it on the bench beside the wood box so that Jibby could sniff it. Then she moved the dish to the floor under the bench.

Jibby daintily circled the piled wood in the box a time or two and then sprang to the floor. She dipped her quick tongue into the bowl. She meowed once and backed away. Stalking haughtily out of the kitchen, she looked into all the downstairs rooms in the front of the house. When she came to the stair well, she turned around and scampered back to the kitchen, where she lapped up all her milk.

After that, Peter took Jibby a pan of milk when he carried breakfast and supper out to the big shepherd in the stable. The puppies still fed at their mother's breast. Jibby kept her warm bed between them, but she nursed less and less, and soon stopped altogether.

She made herself welcome in the farm house. A

package came from the city and Peter's mother opened it in the yellow pool of lamplight on the sitting-room table. A length of string dangled over the edge of the table, and Jibby jumped and grabbed for it with her paws. The swinging end of string invited her to play, and she took possession of it as her own. She reared up on her hind legs and pawed at it busily and joyfully. In a minute her legs were tangled in it, and she rolled over on her back and fought to get free. Even Julius smiled over the top of his farm magazine.

"Peter," said Mrs. Julius, "where is your old red top?"

The boy ran to fetch the shining toy from his hideaway on the low shelf in the dark, slant-ceilinged closet under the stairs. He wound the top with Jibby's piece of string and whipped it into a swift spin in the center of the floor. The startled kitten cocked her little head curiously to one side. Suddenly she leaped and, with one brave blow of her paw, laid the top low. It lay conquered and still. Jibby watched it in suspense, pranced around it two or three times, and touched it with gentle paws.

Jibby cleaned herself long and often, with an air of objective attention. When she was tired, she always sought out the same spot on the bench by the kitchen stove. Sometimes she purred, especially when Peter stopped by the bench and stroked her. She slept there many hours of the day, her nose in the fragrant woodpile. If Peter wakened her, she stretched a little and started to play.

Out in the barn things were more exciting than ever. Her foster brothers were getting too big for Jibby to romp with, although for a little while yet she was easily their match. When they got too rough, she showed her pinsharp claws at them. One morning Jibby felt so full of mischief that she cuffed one of the puppies in greeting. Both of them yelped in concert and rushed her. Jibby lay on her back in the straw, paws limp, feigning weak surrender. The puppies flung themselves on her and collided with each other. Just when they thought they had her down, out of the furry brown and white tangle leaped a gray streak. Jibby was out of reach and halfway along her private catwalk before the dogs could right themselves. They followed her down the length of the barn as far as Midnight's stall. Jibby gained her perch on the ledge and she sat primly licking the fur on her hind quarters while Midnight's snorts kept the dogs at bay.

One evening after supper Jibby had the kitchen all to herself. She was sitting in the square of heat in front of the oven, squinting lazily into space. There came a tiny sound, less than a pin fall or water dripping in the sink. A mouse edged softly out of his hole, froze, and then scampered across the room to nibble at some crumbs that had fallen from the table. He moved in busy silence from crumb to crumb.

Jibby's ears moved up and forward, and her eyes sparkled. Slowly, without a sound, she let herself down on all fours and crouched to spring. The mouse, his back to the kitten, stopped foraging. He did not act frightened yet, or as if he even sensed the approach of the age-old scourge of his race. But he had received an urgent signal of some sort. Then Jibby leaped and pounced in a single movement—a fast, low, exact arc with a full stop at both ends. The mouse dodged Jibby's paw, but now the kitten was crouched between him and his hole. Hypnotized or perhaps merely puzzled, he faced her for two long seconds.

The mouse ran a few tiny steps. Jibby's head, held obliquely, followed every movement, and then she pounced again. The mouse veered and was blocked once more. He took a few last steps on dragging feet—

not to escape but to accommodate the enemy, it seemed—and lay trapped between Jibby's paws. All at once he stopped moving.

Jibby pushed the limp gray ball with her nose, but it did not stir. This hurt Jibby's feelings. For her the game had been too short. At last she picked the mouse up in her teeth and ran into the front room where the family was sitting around the ample library table. She laid her booty on the floor at Peter's feet.

"Mother!" Peter exclaimed, throwing his pencil down on top of his arithmetic tablet and cupping his hands around his kitten's clever head. "Look what Jibby's got!"

"Look, Julius!" his mother echoed.

"Good girl," Julius said in his grave way. "That's fine. Now you are beginning to earn your keep."

From then on nothing was greater fun for Jibby than the mouse hunt. She went sniffing for them all over the house and barn. She memorized every mouse hole she found. She lay alert and unmoving for half an hour, waiting for a small gray head to poke itself out of one hiding place or another. She kept a sharp watch on the pantry. Her greed for mice mounted.

One day she trailed Julius to the lower corn field.

Under his arm he had slung a shotgun to shoot the crows that swooped down to peck at the new stand of grain. At first the noise routed Jibby. Her ears flattened, her eyes squinted, and, tail curved under her body, she streaked back to the house. Afterward, though she kept farther behind him, she went along when she saw him hobble the horses at the barn and fetch his gun. Soon she could hear a lot of shooting without running away, and one day she was rewarded for her curiosity and her good nerves. Julius fed her some torn bits of the raw bird flesh, which Jibby swallowed down with gusto.

Jibby was content. She gorged herself on milk and crow's meat, carried on her delicious battle with the mice on Julius' farm, and accepted as her proper due the love and praise of the boy Peter.

It was mid-morning, and Midnight's stall was full of people. Jibby watched it all from her perch on the ledge just above the bull's feeding trough. Not only Julius, but Peter and his mother were gathered around the bull. Midnight hung his head and occasionally let out a bellow that had more pain than threat in it.

Jibby's nose twitched. A strange man in a dark suit

and a straw hat, carrying a small black leather satchel, was entering the barn. While the family stood around outside the stall, he tapped Midnight's sides and bent over to feel the bull's legs.

All at once Jibby's ledge seemed less safe. The new man had stood outside for a long while talking with Julius and shaking his head from side to side. Now the two men were forcing something between Midnight's teeth. Jibby rose with arched back and prepared to flee. The bull's hind hoofs splintered the little swing-door to his stall. Afterward they brought Flora and Sara's blankets and buckled them over Midnight's broad back.

Then they all went away. Peter did not even notice when Jibby rubbed against his leg in a vain appeal for attention. It was very strange, since nobody in Lady's corner had been given anything to eat that morning.

Night came, but no supper. Lady had dug up an old bone and was indifferent. Jibby and the two puppies filed out of the barn and paraded into the kitchen, meowing and yelping now at Peter, now at his mother. Nobody gave them any milk or scraps. Worse, Mrs. Julius waved her long black apron in their faces and shooed them out into the yard.

Jibby returned to the barn, but not to Lady's corner. A lighted lamp hung crookedly on a nail against the side of Midnight's stall, and Jibby peeked in. Something stopped her from going close. The bull was a stranger too. His snorts came fast and his eyes rolled in his head, but every time he stamped a hoof he staggered. He lashed out feebly at a dragging corner of one of the blankets, lurched sideways, and went down on his front knees in the straw. Jibby streaked to the haymow.

She padded silently to the spot where the square of dim light from the high front window met the edge of the towering mound of hay in the center of the floor. She dug out a little cave for herself in the hay. Lying down facing the trapdoor, she stared at Peter's pitchfork where it leaned against the wall. Hungry as she was, she went to sleep.

Jibby was awake and waiting long before dawn, when she stalked and killed a field mouse in the hayloft. She was busy eating it when Peter climbed the loft ladder to pitch hay down to the horses and cows. She did not drop her breakfast to scamper at his heels, and Peter did not pause in his work to stroke and praise her.

It got dark and light again before Jibby descended

to the barnyard and caught a bird. Once during the night, Jibby had stood at the edge of the trapdoor and looked down across the barn under the hanging lantern. The bull lay on his side looking very thin, stiff, and bony. His legs stuck out like four straight sticks. His neck was stretched long and flat, and his eyes were shut as if he were sleeping.

In the morning they found Midnight dead in his stall. Peter hung his head and went blindly about his chores. Suddenly he caught up a spade that stood beside the oat bin and rushed out of the barn, almost trampling Jibby who was on her way in from break-fasting on a blackbird. Jibby wailed, but the boy trudged on without turning.

"Peter!" his mother called sharply after him.

Catching up with Peter in the orchard, Jibby sat on her haunches and watched the boy begin to re-move the sod between two spreading apple trees. The spade bit deep into the clay.

"Peter!" The shout came from the barn, where Julius stood in the door, waving the boy to come in. Peter sighed, stood the spade upright in the earth, and trotted doggedly up to his father.

"What on earth do you think you are doing out there?" Julius demanded harshly.

Peter lifted his gaze as far as the top of his father's work boots and spoke in a very low voice.

"Digging a grave, sir," he said, "for M-midnight."

The last words trailed off in a whisper as his father threw back his head and gave a short, harsh laugh. Rage reddened Julius' face and he clenched one rough hand.

"What a fool!" he shouted to the empty barnyard. "The carcass goes to the blacksmith for his hide and glue, sleepyhead. If you want to be useful, fetch the windlass or hitch up the horses." Julius turned on his heel and started for the house.

"But I thought you loved Midnight," Peter began, his young eyes wide and unbelieving. His mother's hand flew to her mouth but she made no sound.

"Get out of my sight," thundered his father, "and stay out."

Peter's face went suddenly white, and he turned and ran through the barn to the hayloft. His throat burned, and he held his fists clenched at his sides and his body rigid.

Jibby appeared at the top of the steps just as the boy threw himself down in the hay and began to cry. She ran up to her playmate, prepared as usual to settle in his lap and lay her head under his chin.

Peter gave her a push, which Jibby mistook for part of a new game. She scratched his knees and sprang to her proud perch on his shoulder. But Peter, busy with his first grown-up sorrow, knocked her off with a brusk swipe that sent her sprawling.

"Go away, Jibby!" he said, putting his head down on his arms again. But the kitten gave a blow for a blow. Lightning fast her paw raked across the boy's hand, making the blood come. Peter sat up and stared at her, nursing his hand. Jibby did not retreat. She sat spitting at him, paws raised for defense or attack.

Peter forgot that he had fished her out of the cold river. He forgot Jibby was his hard-earned pet. For a moment she was a wildly excited enemy and he her wounded antagonist.

The kitten, still spitting, began to back away. She had seen Peter's face change. He was big and strong, and he looked as if he meant to punish her. Jibby, however, was not one to take punishment. The notion was foreign to her kind. She had seen the dogs cower and whimper under Mrs. Julius' light discipline, but Jibby was not a dog. If she could not win by scratching and spitting, she could run.

Peter caught up with her at the trapdoor. He lifted her roughly by the scruff of the neck and dropped her all the way to the barn floor below. Jibby landed on the planks with a thud and a cry of pain. Then she slowly rose to her feet, arching her back and half turning toward the haymow. Then she relaxed: her babyhood was over. Without a backward look toward her one-time friend and benefactor, she sailed in a graceful curve through the open barn door and took to the open.

CHAPTER III

HUNTING DAYS

J IBBY WAS RUNNING AWAY. Turning her back on
the barn and the river of her childhood, she ran
in the opposite direction—toward the violet haze of
the mountains on the far side of Farmer Julius' valley.

Beyond the lower barn lot lay the big field. Here at the edge of the young corn the farmer used to feed her shreds of fresh crow's meat. Jibby's tail whipped her flanks and lashed the corn stalks on both sides of her path into a dry rattle. Somewhere in the middle of the field she sat down, still so excited that the tip of her tail jerked back and forth. The corn was already high and concealed her like a forest thicket.

At last she calmed down and began to make her toilet. Her tongue washed her breast, belly, and almost all of her back. She licked her paws, scrubbed her face with them, and licked them off again, returning over and over to her head and ears until she felt clean. The battle in the hayloft was almost forgotten. Her nose was pointed toward the wildwood and freedom.

With her breakfast of blackbird far behind her, Jibby was hungry. She snapped up every insect that crossed her path—mere bites that left her more greedy than ever.

Sniffing diligently, she prowled along between the rows of standing corn. A bird fluttered and circled above her, keeping pace with her slow progress but staying out of reach. It was a lark fearful for her brood; and, in spite of herself, she led Jibby on. The cat stood still, pretending to look for a worm and making an elaborate show of ignoring the worried mother. But her ears were stretched to follow the lark's flight. The unhappy bird could not help herself. She led the cat straight to a nest that lay flat and unprotected among the furrows. In it sat four nestlings, holding their bills appealingly open.

Jibby was not touched by the sight, any more than she was deflected from her purpose by the mother hysterically fluttering overhead. She made a feast of all four baby larks, the weak chirping of her victims and the helpless cries of the mother only adding to her zest.

Within the next hour two field mice also fell prey to the huntress in the corn.

At last Jibby came to the far edge of the corn field and stepped out on a wagon road where the sun shone hotly. It was little more than three tracks down the middle of a broad strip of grass running between Julius' stand of corn and the edge of a big wood. The warm grass was like a caress, and Jibby curled up lazily in the sun and fell sound asleep.

She was awakened at sundown by the sudden chill. The sun was gone from the road, though a little red-gold light rested among the treetops across the way. Jibby looked around for some kind of cover and trotted off down the road until she came upon a low shed. It was built with one whole side open to the forest. Inside somebody had piled several cords of firewood. Jibby fitted herself into a niche between the top of the pile and the eaves. Once in the night she was awakened by the woodchuck whose home she had usurped. He took one look at his uninvited guest and turned at bay. He bared his fierce little teeth, whistled with terror and rage, and fled back into the forest. Jibby, who had barely opened her eyes during the encounter, went straight to sleep again, feeling safer than ever. But she was awake and prowling the road for breakfast before the sun came up. On the farm side of the road, the field of corn gave way to a stand of waving wheat.

A soft but powerful whir of wings made her stop in her tracks. She sat down on her haunches and looked skyward. A king pheasant was skimming over the grass at the forest's edge, heading for the field of grain. He was a beautiful sight for a cat to see. From tip to tail his coat of feathers made a rich design of glowing color. Jibby gazed in awe at his neck, where the feathers gleamed like dark blue metal. The big bird wheeled down and settled in the grass between the road and the wheat. He took several quick running steps along the edge of the grain, stopped, and ran a little farther. Jibby continued to watch him. And suddenly her mouth watered, for her nose had caught his scent. She was also very hungry.

Jibby ran across the road behind the promenading pheasant and began to stalk him. With a slow fanning of his wide wings, the bird rose indolently in the air and dropped down into the wheat near by. Jibby slipped in after him. The grain opened to receive her, hissing melodiously. But her bird had flown. However there was more than one pheasant in the field. Here and there one would lift itself in the air with a rush of wing noises, and Jibby would dash after him, but at no time did she come close enough to her prey to pounce. Her appetite grew.

Finally one of the birds in its flight led her back into the roadway again, and there was a mother quail sedately walking the open road at the head of her covey of chicks. Jibby promptly caught and ate the earth-bound quail.

Jibby felt like herself again, carefree and sleepy. The fragrance of the dewy road and fields, the sharp woods smell, the scent of mice and birds, caressed her nostrils. The pheasants no longer tempted her. Jibby curled up for a well-earned nap.

But adventure and danger come unbidden.

From up the road a man came strolling. A dainty little wire-haired fox terrier pranced beside him. Jibby, sleepy no longer, mistook him for a puppy; and with puppies Jibby had had only the best of relations. She lifted her head from her paws, sat up on her haunches, and with pleasant suspense prepared to welcome a new playmate.

"Sic 'em!" said the strange man. Neither the words nor the tone had Jibby ever heard before, so she did not pay much attention. "Sic 'em, Terry! Get her."

The terrier rushed forward, and Jibby was overrun so violently that she rolled off the low slope into the road. The terrier did not wait for her to get up. He was on top of her, growling in grim earnest. He snapped at her furiously. His teeth bit her forelegs and back painfully.

Lithely she slipped out from under him and took her stand opposite him, spitting with hate. The ignorant terrier moved in to attack again.

A blow from Jibby's paw caught his nose, and he pulled back yelping. Jibby let loose a rain of blows all aimed at the dog's eyes. He dodged left and right and tried to strike back, but Jibby tore a row of bloody stripes across his forehead. The terrier howled in pain.

The man lifted his cane. Jibby saw his gesture before he could interfere. Like a streak she gained the edge of the wood and ran in among the trees. The dog did not pursue her. But she ran on in aimless excitement.

A splash of sunlight ahead drew her to a grassy clearing. The trees had been cleared from it long ago, and the floor was like a level lawn. It was about a hundred yards long and half as wide, with a small shed about the height of a man at one end. There was a heavy padlock on the door and the tiny windows were too high for Jibby to reach. It was a shooting range where the forester and game warden came once a month or so to keep in practice. Today nobody was there, and the guns and targets were locked in the shed.

Jibby settled herself in the middle of the smooth lawn where the sun poured through the opening in the trees. There she gave herself a thorough washing, while she pondered the question of dogs. Some were harmless playmates and good comrades; others were treacherous enemies. From now on she would have to be on her guard whenever she met one. The best course was instant flight; but, if she were cornered, she would attack first.

Jibby awoke suddenly. A biting scent was drifting up her nose. Immediately she was alert, arching her back and looking around. There it was. A fox, not yet aware of Jibby, was slinking along the edge of the clearing, where he had just had a long drink at the brook.

Equally startled, the fox and the cat confronted each other. Jibby, who had never met a fox before, took him for a dog. She spat menacingly.

The fox opened his ugly jaws and rushed at her. A wave of his scent hit Jibby in the face and almost knocked her down. In fear and panic she vaulted clear over the fox. Then she fled. There was no question, she knew, of standing battle against this enemy. He was more than a dog; he was a wild and dangerous animal bent on murder.

Behind her she heard the branches of the underbrush rattle against each other. The fox was in pursuit and gaining ground. Without pausing in her flight, Jibby headed straight for a large beech tree and leaped. Landing halfway up the trunk, she clung to it for a moment and scrambled higher. She gained the first wide bough and stealthily she made her way upward until she was hidden in the beech's thick green crown. A new fear assailed her, and she looked back to see if the murderer was climbing too.

But the fox only leaned his forepaws against the trunk and growled impotently up into the branches. And at last with a disgusted blink of his crafty eyes he trotted away. Before he was quite out of sight, he stopped, looked back, and, with a flick of his brush, resumed his brisk trot. Jibby watched him vanish into the thicket.

Jibby crouched where she was without moving. It was a long time before she caught her breath and relaxed. The thick limb to which she clung had a twin, and where they joined the main trunk they offered her slender body a secure and comfortable bed. Slowly she stretched herself all over. After turning around several times, she lay down and peered into the leafy branches above, below, and on every side of her.

Birds were flying in and out of the green cathedral in which she had found sanctuary, and Jibby was famished.

She slipped here and there, from branch to branch. A bluejay caught sight of her and let out an angry cry. The woodpecker had nothing but an ironical laugh for her. There were finches and robins, but they came nowhere near; besides, they were too fast. A squirrel sped by like lightning.

This was a good place. There were delicious tidbits up among the treetops. Jibby lay in wait. She did not move: only the tip of her tail quivered.

Again the squirrel passed by. He sat up delicately, balanced against his tail, his short forepaws laid devotionally close against his white breast. Jibby gave the little creature no time to be afraid or to flee. There was a short squeak, and the cat had bitten the squirrel's throat through and through.

After this refreshment, Jibby went back to her bed against the beech trunk and washed herself all over. Evening came, but she did not go to sleep. A new excitement had entered Jibby from the surrounding forest. It was the excitement of the hunt coupled with the knowledge of the hunter. She sensed that the birds had to sit in their nests when the silence of the night brought sleep to their eyes. On the wing they mocked her; in their nests it would be a different story. Jibby schemed to grab the sleeping birds one after another. There would be good hunting and plenty to eat in the dark.

A loud cackling arose in the woods—a shrill *gocking* followed by a soft chuckle—and drew nearer and nearer to Jibby's hiding place. And now the air was thick with the soft, heavy beat of many strong wings —not one pheasant but a whole colony of the succulent birds was wheeling toward Jibby's part of the forest. She did not stir, watching and listening tensely, the end of her tail twitching. By twos and by threes they settled in the trees all around her. Her own beech was one of the pheasants' roosts. Jibby settled down comfortably to wait for the dark and a supper of pheasant.

She thought of the fox standing on his hind legs and reaching as far as he could up the tree trunk, and jeered to herself. She was in command up here. She reigned over an empire of pheasants and squirrels quite safe from the fox, who could not climb a tree.

Night fell over the forest. An owl floated by in eerie flight, perfectly light and perfectly noiseless. And in a moment her melancholy call drifted back. "Whoo-oo-ah," she sang, sad and mysterious, in tune with the pulsing blackness.

The sounds of the night forest gathered momentum. It whispered, it crackled, it rustled. Suddenly a loud cry splintered the night.

"Oi yeek! Oi yeek!" it came, shrill and near and nerve-wracking, as if somebody were on the point of death. It brought Jibby up on her feet in a nervous crouch, ears pointed, ready for flight. The blood-curdling yell came again, from the direction of the tall pine tree at the edge of the little clearing; and Jibby made out the cause of this new terror. It was the screech-owl, a harmless puff of white and tan feathers sitting far out on a solitary limb that reached halfway to Jibby's clump of beeches. He was chuckling into his beard. The forest took up its interrupted murmuring. A small bird a foot above Jibby's head chirped in its sleep.

Jibby sank back in her corner. The idea of seizing a pheasant and overpowering it as it slept, worked in her like a fever.

Finally she arose and explored the two branches that met to form her resting place. Neither harbored a pheasant. She climbed one branch higher, passing close to two roosting birds without seeing them. They were hidden beneath a screen of leaves hanging low from the boughs above them, and each one had tucked himself together to look like a knot of wood in the darkness. Jibby ranged the next branch to the very tip, where it lay against the thick limb of a neighboring beech. She slipped across without making a sound or stir and almost bumped her nose into a pheasant asleep with his head under one wing. He was bigger than she had thought.

One swift bite, and his hot blood streamed over her nose. The big bird made no struggle, no outcry. With scarcely a tremor, he slid from sleep to death.

Methodically Jibby tore her catch to pieces and began to feast. She ate fast at first and then more slowly; but half a pheasant was enough to gorge her. For a little while she kept on pecking at it and then she could not swallow another bite. She left the rest where it lay and moved sluggishly away from the scene.

She did not return to her corner in the beech tree. She was already too cunning a marauder for that. Neither did she risk a descent to the forest floor. Instead she picked her way slowly from tree to tree, licking up the fresh dew from the leaves as she passed and leaping from one interlacing bough to another until she landed in a giant sycamore. Here she found a level nook among the lower branches where a gnarled elbow gave her plenty of room and shelter. Like the pheasants, she chose a place where some upper branches made a natural screen for her bed.

When morning dawned Jibby did not stir. The forest resounded with the sweet songs of the blackbird and the thrush, the gay strophes of the finches and robins, the whispering of the titmice, the loud scolding of the magpies, the jubilation of the orioles, and the discordant cawing of the crows. The cackling pheasants wheeled down from their sleeping trees and made off for their feeding grounds.

None of it reached Jibby's ears. She lay on her snug bed in the sycamore and slept all day long.

The crows and the magpies, spying the remains of the slaughtered pheasant, gathered around it for a meal. They argued and battled and, among them, cleaned up the last shred. Only a few bright feathers that drifted down to the ground and blew around among the leaves bore witness to the feast.

On the forest floor below, the landowner and his game warden, guns slung in the crook of their arms, paused in their morning patrol. The forester spied a glistening tail feather.

"Look here," he called to his companion, pointing with his gun to other bright flecks of blue and gold on the path. In the air above them a handful of lighter feathers drifted about under the beech limb. "Hawk killed a pheasant," he added. "Or maybe a marten."

"Keep a sharp watch for a day or two," the other man said, "and you'll catch the villain red-handed."

Jibby remained unhearing and invisible. Her striped coat blended with the mottled bark of the sycamore.

Toward evening she awoke full of life again and ready for a night's sport. She groomed herself and watched the sun sink below the tops of the trees. As dusk fell, she heard the distant clucking of the pheasants, and then they flew up in a cloud. Their wings filled the air all around with sound and motion.

At the height of the stir, Jibby descended from her sycamore for a drink at the brook. She had been nagged by thirst all afternoon, and the stream purling along at the edge of the little clearing had drawn her like a magnet. But she was afraid of the fox who drank there. She had kept a sharp lookout, and seen him come from the direction of the road. He had stopped at the water's edge and then trotted off into the thicket. Now she felt safer with all the racket overhead. A squirrel came along and drank beside her. Jibby's nose twitched, but she saved her appetite for the pheasants. Wasting no time, she was soon back on her perch in the sycamore tree.

When it was pitch dark, she slipped light-footedly through the trees on the prowl for the dark clumps that were now her special game. For a short moment she squatted beside a solitary bird, savoring in advance the pleasure of the kill. But not for long: a short pounce, a quick, fatal bite—and the rich, leisurely meal lay before her.

Night after night Jibby killed a pheasant, and each day she slept until afternoon. Her fur grew heavy and long. The rich diet added gloss and color to her striped coat. Its background of gray turned darker. Black stripes ringed her body from tip to toe and even ran in circles round her fine long tail. There was an hour at high noon when the sun shone directly down on her perch, but she never awoke until it had left her and moved on. After her grooming, she ranged the sycamore and lay down wherever she found the most sun. The fox trotted by. The pheasants wheeled home, and Jibby drank at the spring that flowed past the little clearing. No one used the shooting range and, if the warden was hanging about, Jibby was the one creature in the whole woods that never saw him.

One evening the moon appeared—a narrow sickle in the bright evening sky. Then a half-moon rode high in the starry night as Jibby jumped from tree to tree on her way to dinner. Finally the full moon lighted up the whole forest.

The game warden had been patrolling the sleeping

grounds ever since the half-moon, looking for signs of a marten. One cloudless, moon-drenched night, having delayed his coming until the moon was up, he spied a small creature crouching near one of the laden boughs. Certain he had the marauder, he raised his gun and fired.

To Jibby's sharp ears, it sounded like the snap of a whip. Then she felt the blow. A piece of buckshot had buried itself in her thigh. She sprang to another branch; but the sting in her thigh was not left behind. The tiny wound burned like fire. Carefully, limping on three paws, Jibby made her way back to the sycamore. Shaking with terror, she squatted in her corner and began licking the hole in her leg where the shot had gone in. She kept up a steady licking hour after hour. But the pain of the wound went on; it grew worse. Panic told her to run; weakness bade her stay quiet.

Late in the night a certain creature approached and stood in front of her, sniffing inquisitively. It was the curious marten, come to pay a call. Jibby sensed her visitor was weighing whether to attack or start a peaceful conversation. But she did not wait for him to decide. She spat angrily, lifting her forepaws in a wild threat.

[57]

The marten did not move. It was the first time he had ever seen a creature like Jibby at close range.

"Where do you come from?" he grunted agreeably.

"None of your business!" Jibby spat back.

"Why are you so angry?"

"It hurts."

"Where?"

Jibby showed her caller her wound.

"Oh," nodded the marten sagely, "the firehand, isn't it?"

"Firehand?" asked Jibby. "The thing that makes a loud noise? Nonsense!"

"All the two-leggers have them," the marten murmured.

"Don't talk nonsense," scolded Jibby. "The man had a rifle."

"Call it a rifle for all I care." The marten sounded gloomy.

Jibby had a dim picture of a man shooting crows. The racket had always come first and bird flesh later. But now, no tidbits: only the pain.

"I know these men well," she boasted. "I stayed with them a long time."

The marten advanced a step.

[58]

"Tell me," he said, sitting down companionably across from Jibby on the wide sycamore bough, "what are they like?"

Jibby considered.

"At times, nice," she stated. "But in the end, bad."

"Here in the forest," said her caller, "they are only bad. They are a great danger to us."

"This—" Jibby snarled, lifting her wounded thigh for the marten to see.

"That was meant for me," said the marten. "It was me he intended to murder."

"Stuff and nonsense!" Jibby answered. "I'm the one he hurt."

But the marten refused to fight over the honor.

"I am very sorry," he said. "These full-moon nights— At such times our kind must be very careful."

"I'm not yet at home here in the forest," Jibby said. I am not very expert—"

"You are learning."

"Learning," Jibby sighed. "If I don't starve in the meantime!"

"You won't starve so easily."

"Bring me something to eat, my friend," Jibby begged.

"I?" The marten grinned. "I bring you something? I'll be happy to find something for myself a night like this."

"Just a scrap," Jibby whined.

The marten gave his disagreeable laugh.

"Have you any idea of my hunger, little one?" he said. "You're lucky I don't eat you."

Jibby spat wildly and lifted a forepaw ready to scratch at the marten's eyes.

"I don't want anything to do with you one way or another," grumbled the marten. Turning away, he silently vanished.

During the days that followed Jibby lost weight rapidly. Her leg hurt and she was famished all the time. If she was also afraid, her fear had no object. Nevertheless, her wound healed almost completely, and one day she could get up and look for something to eat. But her thigh was stiff as if with an echo of the first sharp pain, and she limped.

The halcyon nights were over. Jibby hunted smaller prey than pheasant. Not only hunger drove her. Mixed with it was anger, as if she hated her puny victims for not being plumed and kingly. She played gruesomely with every creature she caught, relishing each moment of the losing struggle of magpie or jay, forest mouse or squirrel, before she decided to finish off her prey.

To Jibby's new horror the leaves were falling from the trees. The deer roaring and battling up and down the forest caused her no alarm. But the falling of the leaves that ran like a gentle, steady whisper through the woods made her uneasy.

Next the nights turned cold. This was something Jibby could not stand; her whole body trembled. An icy storm roared down on the forest, blowing the dead leaves before it in dancing swirls. Soon the sycamore was stripped bare, and the other trees stood stark naked. So Jibby had to descend to the ground.

One night when it was pitch dark she crept down into the low brush, where at dawn she stalked and killed a large hare. It was pleasant not to be hungry, and she slept: but not calmly. She changed her place many times. More than ever, now that she was handicapped by her stiff thigh, she feared to meet her old enemy, the fox.

Cold and hunger finally drove her to set out to look for shelter with some human beings. Day after day she scouted far and wide up and down the forest. Deep in the forest one day she entered a high, quiet meadow in the center of which was a charcoal burner's hut. But no one came in answer to her repeated meows. She took a wide forest trail that led up out of the high meadow, and came upon the game warden's lodge. The pretty cottage in its tiny garden was perched on the wooded slope where the forest met the mountains that rimmed the valley. Jibby had wandered to the farthest reaches of the wildwood, a long way indeed from the little clearing by the beech grove.

To Jibby a house meant warmth, milk set out in a dish, and caresses. Confidently she ran up the garden path. Two big dogs bounded out to meet her, snarling. The warden ran out too, rifle in hand.

Jibby headed for the nearest thicket, one of the dogs close in pursuit. The cat turned and slapped him. Muzzle bleeding, the dog backed away. In one plunge Jibby was deep in the thicket, the uproar lost behind her.

Keeping to the heavy cover of the underbrush, she crept back through the forest. There seemed never to be an end to danger. She stopped only to nourish herself now and then, meagerly, on a mouse. She feared the fox too much now to stalk better game. She slept fitfully and only when she grew weak with fatigue. Keeping an eye out for the fox, she followed the brook down past the beech grove and her old sycamore tree to the little clearing.

At last she reached the open again. A broad field of stubble and corn shocks lay before her eyes, the inhospitable forest at her back. The night of her return from the wildwood Jibby slept in the wood shed by the road and, when morning came, she took up her watch for a protector.

CHAPTER IV

BACK TO CIVILIZATION

ALL DAY LONG Jibby kept her watch by the road, crouching in the soft earth of a plough trench under the shelter of a rustling corn stock. Toward mid-afternoon she heard voices. Two men came walking down the road. Luckily neither man carried a rifle or even a walking stick.

Jibby picked her way along the furrow and out upon the dry grass shoulder bordering the wagon tracks. The men tramped by. They both saw her but made no sign. Jibby fell in behind them and limped along at their heels.

"Meow!" cried Jibby, begging for attention.

"Victor," said Julius, "a cat's following us." He gave his leg a shake as Jibby rubbed against his high heavy boot.

His companion came to a stop.

"Julius!" he exclaimed. "Don't do that. Can't you see the poor thing is hurt?" He bent down and picked Jibby up in his arms. "Why, poor little kitty!" he crooned.

In answer to the gentle tone, Jibby purred loudly and snuggled on his chest. The man stroked her, and to Jibby it seemed she had found everything she was looking for. She went on purring.

"Fresh from a fight with a marten over a fat pheasant," said Julius, looking over the schoolmaster's head into the forest alongside. "Looks disreputable enough," he teased.

"You're too hard on animals," Victor said.

Jibby kept on purring.

They walked on toward the crossroads, Victor cradling the cat in his arms.

"Are you going to take it home with you?" Julius demanded.

"Yes," said Victor in a quiet voice. "Don't you hear it purr?"

"I'm not deaf," said the farmer sharply. "So what?"

"All right, call it an act if you like," said the teacher. "To me it's a sign of confidence."

"Oh, I believe it feels well," scoffed Julius. "Quite centered on itself."

Victor laughed. At the crossroads, he set Jibby down. Jibby watched them stride on up the wide main road away from her, and the fear of the open took hold of her again. She hobbled hastily and in silence after her new friend.

They filed along for a hundred yards or so, and the schoolmaster glanced back. He gave a chuckle and waited. Then he picked the cat up.

"Humph!" snorted the farmer.

The two neighbors walked on in the silence old friends keep—past Julius' barn until they halted in front of the teacher's house.

"I wonder," said Julius, "how your dog will treat your tramp cat."

"Come and see for yourself," Victor said, one hand on the open gate. "Drop in after the milking's done," he called as Julius turned back toward his big red barn.

Victor pushed open the front door with his foot.

"Look what I've got," he shouted toward the back of the house. He put Jibby down on the bare hardwood floor of his study. The schoolmaster liked the austerity of the bare floor. Besides, this way he could have his pets inside the house without making extra work for Pauline, his wife. A wood floor was easier to keep clean than a carpet.

He had laid the new floor in himself two summers ago, planning and matching each strip of hickory or ash as if he were working with gold and silver. It had been a labor of love and beauty. A great five-pointed star, inlaid in the darker hickory, decorated the whole space. Then he had given it a one-inch grade from walls to center. In the middle, under his ample work desk, he had drilled a hole through the board and fitted it with a wire drain.

Twice a week Pauline brought in a pail of hot soap suds and her older broom, and scrubbed to her heart's content. As a last touch, she rinsed it all over with cold spring water from the well in the front yard, sweeping toward the middle of the floor. The water ran off through a waste pipe fitted underneath.

Lately Pauline had begun talking about a new floor just like it for her kitchen.

At Victor's shout, Tasso bounded into the study from the back of the house. He looked like a story-book teddy bear, but he was the brave descendant of a noble line of otter hounds. Jibby arched her back and spat at the shaggy red-brown, gray-brindled giant with sharp pointed teeth in an iron jaw. Tasso worked his bushy amber eyebrows and gave the newcomer a friendly sniff or two.

A strong swimmer, unfailing hunter, deadly fighter and peaceable citizen, Tasso was a full member of the household. He sat down and Jibby marched provocatively around him, her tail lifted straight up like a candle. The short half-curl of Tasso's tail wagged a little.

Victor looked toward the kitchen. Pauline, a tall blond girl with a serene face, her still figure draped in a white cotton blouse and ankle-length black cotton skirt and red-embroidered white apron, stood watching from the doorway. Without a word, Pauline looked at the circling cat and the huge dog.

"Why shouldn't they be friends?" said Victor, his eyes smiling into his wife's. "The enmity between dogs and cats is one part original jealousy and nine parts baiting by people. For centuries we've been driving the animals against each other."

"Maybe you're right," said Pauline. She brought a bowl of milk from the kitchen and put it on the floor. Jibby drank greedily, Tasso looking on amiably as if he were the host.

Jibby looked around the room. In one corner by the fireplace lay a neat square of mattress. A year ago Pauline had found it at a farm sale and cut it down to the right size for Tasso. Jibby hurried to it, sprang upon the exact middle of the fine bed, and sank at once into a deep sleep. Now she had a home. Her troubles were over—no more foraging for scant food, no icy wind, no fox.

The otter hound lay down on the floor beside his mattress and rested one paw on its edge. It was a gentle, strong paw that meant to watch over his guest's slumber. Pauline gave a little shrug as if to say, *Now, what do you think of that?*

Then her eyes went to Victor's as a heavy tread sounded on the path. She giggled, and then turned a serene face to greet Julius at the door.

The farmer took two steps into the study and stopped, staring at the cat that had usurped the dog's place. His face reddened with anger.

"Fine way to reward the best dog in the valley," Julius stormed, pointing an accusing finger at Tasso.

[69]

The otter hound, his.paw steady on the side of his bed, quietly wagged his tail.

"Why do you dislike my cat so much?" Victor asked.

"You know why," said Julius. "I can't stand cats because they are deceitful and tricky. Even cat lovers admit that."

"Look, Julius!" The schoolmaster's tone was grave. "You or I may be these things because we know better. But not my cat. Now, egotism," he went on smilingly, "is something else. Every living thing has a God-given right to be self-centered."

"My dog is no egotist," Julius retorted.

"Oh, yes, she is. Only in a different way—her own way."

"Victor! How can you say that a dog's devotion—"

"Do you beat Lady?" Victor put in.

"Of course—when she deserves it."

"Well, then! I say your dog avoids beatings. She is good to herself."

Julius' mouth tightened.

"I say she is obedient, faithful," he said slowly.

"Right!" Victor nodded. "Dogs are obedient and faithful because that is what assures them a pleasant life."

"Their only motive, you think?"

"No. There is something else." The teacher's glance found Tasso's beautiful eyes across the room. "They love human beings. A dog's master is his god."

"So for once you agree with me," Julius exclaimed. "We are their masters. They live for us."

"They live"—Victor frowned—"for themselves first."

"And, whatever the reason, I guess you will say it's beautiful," Julius scoffed.

"True enough," Victor chuckled, with a sideways glance at his wife to catch her fleeting smile.

Julius began pacing up and down the long room, his hands in his pockets.

"Show me, Victor," he challenged, "that such an animal minds you. Then you'll prove to me that I am wrong."

"But do you demand obedience of every animal?" Victor asked.

"I do—if it wants to live in my house."

Very deliberately Victor lighted his pipe.

"I never demand obedience," he said. "Tasso obeys me anyway. It's been bred in his race for thousands of years. The cat is the only free, proud, uncompromising domestic animal we have. That, at least for me, is her fascination."

"I might as well be fascinated by a cow that refuses to give milk." The husky farmer threw his head back and roared at his own joke. Victor and Pauline laughed with him.

"All right, Julius," said the schoolmaster. "A cat is a free-born creature. Cows can be worked. Dogs can be abused. But a cat puts us on our good behavior. Then she will be friends with us."

"Rubbish!"

"Any relationship with human beings other than equality," the other went on, "is impossible for the cat."

"Friends with a cat!" Julius grumbled disgustedly, turning away from his friend and appealing to Pauline. She shrugged her shoulders and smiled back at him on her way to the kitchen.

"Well, professor," Julius said. "I'm listening. Give me one good reason for this comic love of yours for the whole useless breed."

"I'll give you two," his friend answered. "In the first place, the cat is the aristocrat of the whole domestic animal kingdom. Take the matter of cleanliness. Alley cat, tramp, or pampered queen in the parlor, she is born fastidious. We can't even say that for our own young."

Julius was listening now.

"Yes, professor," he nodded. "If you have to have them around, I suppose it's some help that they are clean."

"But it is more than that," Victor said. "They are royal—the blood of the king of beasts runs in their veins. I see my cat move: her elegant, swinging, almost weightless walk; her precise, wingèd leap. Watching her, I seem to see the big cats—a tiger, a lion, a panther—cross my humble study. She touches my workaday life with splendor—"

Julius' face grew red and he snatched up his hat from the desk.

"What next!" he exclaimed.

"Stay for supper?" Victor called, following him to the door.

"You're crazy," Julius growled and left.

As the door clicked to behind the irate farmer, Jibby woke up. Ignoring everybody, she sat up and, turning her back on Tasso, began to wash herself all over.

After supper that night Tasso made the sleeping arrangements.

[73]

At ten o'clock, Victor knocked out his pipe and began stacking the exercise papers he had been correcting. Tasso took his nose off the schoolmaster's knee and crossed to his mattress. He sank down upon it, forepaws outstretched and head up, waiting for the cat. Jibby was stalking along the far wall, hunting the baseboard for traces of mice. Tasso patiently waited for his guest to finish her round. But Jibby, instead of coming back to the mattress, turned in her tracks and crept back toward the dark hole of the kitchen doorway. Tasso watched her patiently until he saw her poke her nose around the door jamb.

He sprang lithely across the space between them and grabbed the fold of skin on top of her neck firmly in his powerful jaws. He carried her like a dangling dish rag over to their corner and laid her down on the mattress, resting a heavy paw on her body to keep her there. After a moment the cat lay quiet and looked up at him.

Never lifting the paw that held her fast, Tasso climbed up and stretched out beside her on the mat. When she wriggled, he raised his paw a little. Jibby got up, turned around twice, and lay down again, curling herself up against Tasso's wooly flank. The dog heaved a great sigh.

Victor, who had watched them with bated breath, gave an answering sigh and turned out the light.

Early the next morning, Pauline was making apple jelly in her kitchen. Glancing out through the open back door, she caught a glimpse of Julius' son, young Peter, racing along the lane that ran past the bottom of the garden.

"Peter," she sang out from the doorway. The boy stopped and waved his cap. "Come here, will you?" she called, waving the schoolmaster's lunch pail over her head. Peter vaulted over the hedge and ran up to the door.

"My, I'm glad I caught you," Pauline said. "Your teacher forgot his dinner and he's probably halfway to the village by now. I was just thinking I'd have to send Tasso with it." She saw the boy glance in toward the study door. "Come in for a minute," she added. "I want to show you something. We have a new pet."

Peter shyly followed her inside and together they crossed the study over to the mattress.

"A strange cat from the forest," said Pauline. "She has black stripes."

The boy squatted down and put out a hand to stroke the cat.

"Jibby," he whispered as if to himself, but Pauline caught the word. The cat made no sign; she neither spat nor purred. All memory of her former master was gone.

Peter dropped his hand to his side and sat back on his heels.

"We don't know what her name is," Pauline said. "You don't know where she comes from, do you?"

"No, ma'am," Peter said solemnly, hanging his head a little lower, "but—"

"But you think 'Jibby' would be a nice name for her? Is that it, Peter?" Pauline prompted. "We'll call her Jibby."

"I'll be tardy," the boy said, snatching up the dinner pails, his own and Victor's. From the door to the back garden, he gave Pauline a blazing smile.

So, Jibby got her name back, although the schoolmaster and his wife would no more pry into a child's secrets than they would question a cat's decision.

CHAPTER V

THE TAMING OF JIBBY

TWO WEEKS WENT BY. Victor and his wife minis-
tered to Jibby's comfort, letting her do what
she wanted, petting her only as long as she purred her
consent. Victor watched her catch a mouse now and
then, and he was pleased that she paid no attention
to Pauline's chickens.

He suspected that Jibby had already been among

human beings; for a forest cat, she knew too much about civilized behavior. All Pauline had said was that young Peter had named their cat after his lost kitty. But nobody had identified the full-grown tiger cat with the pathetic ball of misery a little boy had once fished out of the river. And Jibby, for her part, ignored the barn and the people next door. Victor felt that Jibby, wherever she came from, belonged with him.

Late one afternoon the schoolmaster stood at the west study window, looking out upon the evening meadows and listening to the soft rustle of the tree-tops. It mingled with the sound of doves declaring their ecstatic tenderness. In the strip of lawn that lay between the house and the river pastures, the doves paraded quietly around.

The neighborhood doves had long ago discovered the charm of Victor's front yard. They spent so much time there that everybody had come to look upon the birds as a part of the schoolmaster's household of domestic animals. Dozens of doves promenaded in and out among the hens that wandered into the front yard from Pauline's chicken run. Normally sedate and busy, the visiting doves would at times turn coquettish. One enamored dove bowed in courtly manner to another, starting the whole flock to cooing and dancing.

Out of the corner of his eye, Victor saw Jibby creeping stealthily around the side of the house. Every line of her graceful body spelled disaster to the doves. Victor hurried outside, but he was too late. Jibby had already struck down a dove. In a kind of shamed conspiracy of silence, doves and chickens alike drifted to the other side of the yard far from the scene of the crime.

Under no circumstances could Victor leave Jibby to enjoy her kill. Yet she wasn't going to easily give up her prey and he was determined not to punish her. Whatever he did now was a gamble on which he staked their relationship.

The man walked toward the cat so that she would see him coming, and softly called her name. At his words and movements, slow as they were, Jibby seized the dying bird in her teeth. But she did not run away. Victor bent down and patted her. Slowly he began to pull the murdered dove from her jaws. Jibby held on tight.

"Jibby! Jibby, be good," Victor murmured soothingly, tugging gently and steadily on the bird. "Give me the dove. Come now, give it to me. You can't do this. It's bad. A good cat doesn't do such things. Now, I'll show you what we'll do."

Jibby's jaws relaxed and the dead dove lay in Victor's palm. He kept on flattering Jibby, patting her lovingly with one hand, while in the other he kept the dead bird before her nose.

"You don't have to eat doves, do you? You may have as many other tidbits as you want. You can catch mice. Rats too, for all I care. There's big game for you! Tasso will take you fishing. Good Jibby. You've been holding yourself in check, haven't you? You never misbehave toward the hens. But the doves? That's backsliding. What do you say, Jibby?"

Jibby crouched motionless, staring above the dead bird in the man's hand.

Victor straightened up and looked down. Still Jibby did not move. Then Victor crossed the yard toward the road, where his shovel leaned against the gnarled apple tree in the fence corner.

"Here, Jibby," Victor called, as he turned up a spadeful of grassy sod.

The cat's eyes followed his every movement as he made ready a small grave for the dead dove. When it disappeared in the earth, Jibby started across the grass, sat down a few feet away, and looked up at him in wide-eyed surprise.

"Yes," he said to her softly, tamping the earth down over the little body and replacing the oblong of sod. It made a little mound. "Isn't it a pity about the poor thing?"

Jibby leaped to his shoulder. She purred loudly, rubbed her head under his chin, and, still purring, let herself be petted. Was she begging for the dove? On the other hand she might be forgiving him.

It was all a bottomless mystery. Victor was playing an endless game in the dark, less conclusive and blinder than the daily one he played in the schoolroom.

With Jibby riding his shoulder, he went to put the spade away in his spacious tool shed. Fetching a sprinkling can, he watered the new grave. Then he set the cat down and, turning his back on her, strolled back to his study. From the window he watched Jibby make her way after him. Not once did she glance toward the busy company of doves and chickens.

In the weeks that followed, his patience was richly rewarded. Jibby never touched a dove again; she passed them by as indifferently as she did the hens.

Victor knew that cats formed habits, many of them

whimsical: even crotchety, like the behavior patterns of very old or very stupid people. But did they have the ability to learn? Did any of the habits result from teaching? He thought not, though it was obvious that cats could be conditioned. They could be induced to adopt new habits, perhaps only to change back without warning. The whole problem of the cat-mind challenged Victor's understanding. He was engaged in a sentimental contest with something he could not put his finger on. In any case, he told himself, if child psychology was his job, cat psychology would be his hobby.

Bright and early Saturday morning one of Victor's younger pupils knocked at the cottage door carrying a yellow canary in a tiny cage. His mother, he said, was sending it as a gift and the bird sang very nicely. A bird in a cage was exactly what Victor did not want. But he could not bring himself to offend the giver. He thanked the boy warmly and spent the rest of the day at the work bench in his tool shed.

He had never·built a cage, least of all one large enough for an eagle. By evening one was ready: four feet square and two feet high at the sides, from which the top rose even higher in a dome.

Now to protect the little singer from the cat. On the advice of Pauline he hung the tremendous cage high on the empty wall across the long study from the fireplace. It swung free from a hook in the ceiling between the two high square windows. They filled the feed bowl with hempseed and put water in the bath. Then Victor stood on a chair to bring the little cage up against the ample door of the big one. In a moment, the canary hopped over the threshold into his new house making a half-smothered peep of delight.

"A canary," Pauline said firmly, "has to be called Hansi."

Hansi began to trill softly. Then he changed to a long-drawn sweet whistling, a wonderful composition of roulades and melodic cadenzas. It mingled with the sunshine inside and out. His tireless singing made the house brighter and spilled over into the sunshine outdoors.

"If it suits you so much in there, little one," said Victor, his eyes held by the tiny throat that swelled with its happy labor, "I am grateful to you indeed— Look at the cat, Pauline," he added in a low voice.

Jibby was listening, but she did not see where the sound came from. Her fur fluffed out a little and her ears flicked around, now toward one corner, now another. Then she must have seen the yellow speck in the big cage. She sped across the room and attempted a big leap. She missed it and fell back again.

"Too short," Victor laughed.

"She'll reach it yet," Pauline said.

Jibby did not repeat the spring and turned away. Victor, watching her subdued but graceful walk, recalled how it is said of lions also that an unsuccessful leap makes them slink away in shame.

Hansi serenaded them from dawn till twilight. He even trilled soft fragments of his song late at night when the hanging lamp above the schoolmaster's desk was lighted. Then Victor had to climb on a high stool and cover the cage with a dark square of silk Pauline fetched from her chest in the bedroom. Victor, however, was not able to thoroughly enjoy his imprisoned pet. It never crossed his mind that the bird was reconciled to his cage; but he grew very fond of Hansi and his singing. The next Saturday, in the morning, he watched Hansi fly all the way around the big cage, and felt a great relief.

At bright noon, however, Hansi's singing came to an abrupt stop. Victor, working in the flower bed under the east windows, heard Hansi's wings flutter in panic. Swiftly Victor slipped around through the kitchen and looked in the study doorway. Jibby was crouched on the roof of the cage. They had not seen her practicing; but finally she had made the leap— maybe from the top of Pauline's rocker, which stood on the same side of the room. Now the cat was attacking the plywood bars with her paws. The little canary huddled on the floor of the cage, head lowered, wings drooping.

Merely to shoo the cat down would not keep her away from the cage another time. The thought of the sling shot flashed across Victor's mind. He used it to chase hawks away from the poultry pen. It was kept in the kitchen cupboard, the sling and a cupful of assorted pebbles. Victor tiptoed to the cupboard and back, planning his strategy.

Jibby must not suspect him. He did not even want her to see the sling shot. If he hit her, he hoped she might link the pain with the roof of the cage, not with a weapon. He hugged the door jamb and took aim. Jibby, absorbed in her mischief, noticed nothing. Victor pulled the string taut and let go. The pebble sped across the study and a cry of fright came from the cat; the stone had hit her square in the flank. Victor, slipping the sling shot in his hip pocket, came in the door.

"What's wrong, Jibby?" he asked, as she dropped to the floor and ran to him piteously. He received her gently. "Anything hurting you?" he added, trying to keep the laugh out of his voice.

Jibby walked all around him with her tail held high, rubbing against his legs. The teacher carried her tenderly out to the yard to be with him and Pauline while they dug up the tulip bulbs.

The rest of the afternoon, Hansi sang no more. Back at his desk right after supper, Victor whistled a bar or two of a waltz. Any other time the canary would have joined in right away. Today he gave only a soft peep now and then.

Pauline and Victor took turns watching Jibby. But the cat kept away from the cage and, so far as they could tell, ignored the little yellow bird. The day Hansi sang out happily again, Jibby lay calmly on Tasso's mattress and made an elaborate toilette. Peace had come back to the study.

Now the winter wind roared around the house and the snow fell. In the study fireplace wood crackled and snapped. The coal range in the kitchen radiated a good glow of heat.

Jibby curled up on the mattress by the study fire or, while Victor was away at the school, sought Pauline's company in the kitchen, stretching out near the stove. As winter advanced, she drew closer to the schoolmaster and his wife.

Toward Tasso, the otter hound, whom the cold had driven into the house for good, she developed a possessive attitude.

Tasso spent a lot of time in front of the fireplace staring into the flames. But, once Jibby began to tyrannize him she would not let him out of her sight. If she discovered him sitting in comfort before the fire, she crouched between his outstretched forepaws. When he grew sleepy and let his head sink down, an upward slap from Jibby warned him to keep his head up. When evening came and it was time to go to sleep for the night, she snuggled into her place against Tasso's flank. But she was not content to lie there as before. She pushed and kicked all night until she lay alone on Tasso's ample mattress in the place his body had warmed.

It seemed that the great dog liked her to rule him. It was as if the new order gave spice to the idle season for them both.

Spring shattered the sleepy silence of the winter world. The first mild night brought with it a company of tomcats to serenade Jibby. The serenade went on all night, a plaint that swelled to a yowling and lasted into the light hours of morning.

Outside in the night, bitter fights developed. Inside Jibby prowled the room—under the windows, before the doors. Then she pled to be let out. Neither Tasso nor Victor even thought of preventing her. And for a couple of nights there were even nosier goings-on. The toms pommeled each other viciously while Jibby paced back and forth among them with a show of innocent aloofness.

At last, however, the tomcats left for good. Ruffled but smugly self-contained, Jibby came back into the house and went to sleep—forever, it seemed. The neighborhood was quiet again.

"Do you think Jibby's body is swelling?" Victor asked Pauline one morning at breakfast.

"Yes," she answered, "she is carrying young. We'll need a proper bed for her now, Victor."

The schoolmaster made a shallow box out of some cold-frames he had bought for the tomato plants. It was about half the size of Tasso's mattress. He covered the bottom of the box with white sand from the river bank. Then he helped himself to some fresh straw from the stack by Julius' barn, and spread a layer of it on top of the sand. Over all this he stretched one of Pauline's discarded sheets and tacked it down to the frame. Jibby's soft, clean bed lay ready for her in the corner left of the fireplace.

"The princess," said Pauline, who had watched all the to-do with amusement, "can be satisfied with that."

Jibby's purr had a new note, part coo and part gentle complaint. The night that she moved to her new bed, Victor kept an eye on Tasso. He was afraid the devoted dog would try to drag the cat back to her old place on the mattress with him. Tasso stalked over, sniffed once, and backed away. Jibby looked ready for battle and at the same time longing and affectionate. The dog gave her a short scolding, just one held-in bark from a few feet away. Then he went and sat for an hour at Victor's knee by the desk.

It was the first night since winter had set in that the otter hound was not crowded out of his own bed by the fire.

Jibby bore her kittens early in the morning, just before Victor had to leave for school. They sent Tasso out into the back yard. They could hear him tearing round and round the house. In rapid succession, one after the other, there appeared three little bodies; and Jibby changed into another cat under their eyes.

With scientific detachment, she washed each cat-child as it came out of her womb and laid it on its side, waiting uneasily for the still-blind kittens to find her breasts. She was gentle, untiring, and patient. She lay on her side, took each little kitten by the neck, and lifted it to her tits. Then, as they took hold, she watched them full of love.

"Well, Jibby," said Victor, bending down to the mother and her kittens, "now you've done it, haven't you?"

She looked at him softly, and he dared to caress her. She was evidently fatigued but she was comfortable. She started to purr.

"Everything's all right," Victor announced in great good humor.

"Of course everything's all right," Pauline said. "A cat like Jibby can stand anything."

The front door latch rattled. It was Tasso coming in. Pauline put out a hand to send him away and Victor glanced at her questioningly.

"She'll scratch him," Pauline warned.

"I wonder. Let him come a little closer," Victor said. "All right, Tasso."

The big dog panted up to Jibby and sniffed the little ones all over. Jibby lifted a languid paw and gently stroked Tasso's muzzle. Victor and Pauline laughed with delight. Tasso wagged his short tail energetically; and Hansi sang, trilled, and fluted.

Two evenings later, as Victor sat reading in an armchair alongside his desk, Jibby came to him holding a young kitten in her mouth. She leaped up into his lap and intrusted her child to him. One by one she fetched the other brother and the sister and laid them too in the teacher's lap. She stood by his knee for a moment fondly watching her brood. Then she leaped up and curled herself around them.

"Now you're all together." Pauline looked up from her sewing. Tasso, wagging his tail, stood as close as he could get and accepted the playful swipes of Jibby's paws.

The kittens grew fast. One was pure white; the second had a smooth yellow coat like a young lioness; and the third was black-striped like his mother. Jibby herself seemed like a kitten again, so untiringly did she frolic with her children, so willingly did she fall in with their droll notions.

Victor neglected his home work. He raided Pauline's work basket for bright-colored wools to wind into a ball. For hours he dangled a ball of wool on a string, enticing the kittens to pounce on the bouncing plaything. He skipped it up and down the floor and kept up the game until Jibby was drawn into it too.

"Four cats!" Julius stood stockstill in the door. Two Saturdays in a row, he and Victor had missed their tramp to the woods. So the farmer came calling. "One, two, three, four," he counted. "What on earth are you going to do with four cats?"

"Nothing, Julius," said Victor, pulling up the armchair for his friend. He held out his tobacco can. "Enjoy them, I guess," he added.

"Aren't you ever going to grow up?" Julius asked, shaking his head. "Don't tell me you are going to keep all four! Why didn't you drown at least two of the kittens right away? You, a humane man!" he scolded.

"Now why should I do that?"

"You have too many, that's why."

"I'm no murderer," Victor said, as if that finished it.

"Stop talking foolishness, Victor. You can't call drowning a couple of new-born cats 'murder'."

"No?" teased the teacher. "What do you call it?"

"I call it—" Julius guffawed and hit his boot top with his hat. "I call it self-defense. Think, man! Think of next spring or next fall." He drew a circle around Victor's desk. "You will have eight or ten cats hopping around here."

"Perhaps." Victor laughed and shrugged. "But that doesn't depend on me. It depends on the cat alone."

"You going to raise every new litter?" Julius got out his pipe.

"Why not? Just look how happy they are to be alive." Victor pointed to the dancing, reeling kittens. The other watched them for a moment.

"You'll come to a bad end yet," he grunted.

Victor chuckled and pointed his pipe stem at Tasso, who was pushing a kitten around with his great paw while Jibby looked on with aplomb.

Julius sat forward on the edge of the chair where he had settled for a minute, watching the new game and now and then glancing sidelong at his peculiar friend.

"You reconcile the bitterest enemies," he said wonderingly.

"I'm not so special," drawled Victor, pulling on his pipe. "It's been done before. How about the sheep dog? Who let the wolf lie down with the lamb? A farmer like you, Julius, who needed a good dog." He held up his hand. "This is a lecture, my friend. Cat and dog? What have I done? I've only looked at old things with new eyes."

Julius tapped out his pipe.

"All right," he said slowly. "Maybe in this case it isn't you that's exceptional, but this cat and this dog."

Victor looked at the animals with new intentness.

"You have it, Julius," he exclaimed, hitting one fist into the palm of the other hand. "Tasso and Jibby —the new-world dog and cat!" He caught up his cap from its hook on the door. "Pauline," he called, "Julius and I are going to walk as far as the woods. Here, Tasso!"

CHAPTER VI

WANDERLUST

IT WAS the hottest day of the summer. Victor carried the yellow canary outside, setting the cage on top of the bird bath. Then he took the three kittens and their mother into the yard for sun and air.

The heat of the sun streamed down and wrapped everything in a sleepy heaviness. Tasso stretched out in the shadow of the house with Jibby asleep close by. The three kittens were lying around half in the generous sun, half in the damp shaded little nooks around the well house. Victor dozed on the sofa inside. Only Hansi the canary was lively. Delighted with the glowing air, the fragrance of the fields, and the brightness of the day, he sang with an excited sobbing threading the melody. His easy trilling made everybody more and more dreamy.

A terrier tore into the yard. He ran toward the lion-colored kitten, and seized it in his mouth. His quick jaws closed over the little neck and crushed it. One short wail escaped from the kitten.

The little dog shook the furry bundle that hung limp in his jaw. His teeth parted, and the yellow kitten dropped to the ground.

The single faint cry had awakened Jibby. But she was barely on her feet when her child dropped lifeless from the strange dog's mouth.

The terrier caught sight of the bristling cat and rushed at her. A blow of her paw threw him back. The terrier recovered himself and closed in, but a rain of slashes from Jibby's paws made him howl with pain. He backed just out of her reach, and stood glowering.

Tasso woke with a growl in his throat and sprang from his place in the little strip of shade against the house. He threw himself against the terrier, who turned a double back-somersault and rolled over. Jibby jumped on top of the floundering terrier. She clung to his back with her savage claws, roweling him till the blood spurted. The terrier rolled over on his back. By this trick he rid himself of the furious cat long enough to spring to his feet and tear away from the scene of battle. Tasso followed him out of the yard and up the river road, barking such horrible curses that the terrier doubled his miraculous pace.

The tumult had brought Victor to the door. At once he reached for Jibby and picked her up in spite of her taut resistance. To calm her, he gathered up the two surviving kittens and showed them to her. Gently she nuzzled the youngsters, sniffed them, and licked their faces once or twice, listening for their soft purrs. For one brief moment, the family united in a muffled purring.

But Jibby was restless and agitated still. She pushed herself out of Victor's arms and ran to the fateful spot where the body of the lion-colored kitten lay. Her voice lifted in a mournful complaint. It took Victor a long time to entice her away. But at last he got her inside and left her licking the two other kittens, while he went to bury their sister in a fence-corner grave beside the dove.

Now in a matter of a few short weeks, Jibby began to neglect her family. One evening Jibby romped with Tasso and turned a deaf ear to her kittens' meows for dinner. The white kitten trailed his tiger-striped brother across the front of the empty fireplace and they tried to find a nook for themselves beside Jibby on Tasso's mattress. Their mother watched them haughtily. Distaste narrowed the elliptical pupils of her eyes. Finally she took the white kitten by the scruff of the neck—and the striped brother in his turn —and deposited them upon their old bed in the farther corner.

"That's funny," Victor said, frowning. "What's happened to her since the yellow kitten died?"

Pauline brought in a dish of milk and knelt on the floor beside the bawling kittens.

"Do you want her to keep on mothering them forever?" she asked, calmly holding first the white kitten and then his gray-and-black brother within tongue's reach of the milk. "Perhaps Jibby is through with the mother business—for this year anyway."

"How can we be sure?" Victor protested. "Do you think she wants to get rid of them? I could take them ın to the school. Just last week the baker's boy was saying he was looking for a kitten."

"Oh," his wife said, "let's wait a day or two. Good boy!" she added as the striped kitten dipped a dainty tongue inside the dish she held in her hand. "I'll have them drinking milk from a dish by then. Besides, I want to see how Jibby does this, don't you?"

"What?" asked Victor crossly. Then he threw back his head and laughed.

"I guess I'm not as keen as you are," he said a little ruefully. "It's against my principles, but I keep wishing she'd show a little of her old feeling for her family. I'm as bad as Julius—"

"Jibby was a beautiful mother," said Pauline serenely. "And I'll never forget the way she sailed into that terrier." She laid the dish of milk beside the kittens and stood with her hands on her hips. "Time to knock down the lying-in bed," she announced. "That old quilt of mine will make a better place for young Tiger and Snowbeard."

Victor nodded and crossed the room to Tasso's mattress. He stroked Jibby's coat. The otter hound leaned his friendly heavy paw on the schoolmaster's shoulder, but Jibby made no sign. She permitted the warm hand to rest on her flank, but she did not purr. Victor sighed and got up to help Pauline change the kittens' bed.

Next day while Victor was away at school, Jibby took her kittens one by one to the tool shed in the back yard and laid them in a high box of gunny sacks. Pauline found them and carried them back into the study. This time they fell upon the dish of milk and lapped it up to the last drop.

It was about five hours later when, on the way home, Victor saw a curious cavalcade coming toward him along the wide road. Jibby stalked on ahead, with the little kittens wobbling and staggering at her heels. Victor stooped in the road and gave each a passing pat as they paraded by toward the river pasture gate. He was telling Pauline about it in the kitchen when they saw Jibby sneak in alone.

It was Tasso who found the lost kittens. He came bounding back from the pasture, two limp kittens bunched clumsily in his jaws. Next morning the teacher set off down the road with a kitten stuffed in each jacket pocket.

Five minutes after the first bell, each kitten had a new home. The baker's boy chose the white kitten; and William, the locksmith's sullen son, asked for Tiger. Victor saw his hand go up but waited, glancing toward the back of the room where young Peter sat at his desk. The farm boy had been watching everything with wistful eyes. Now he dropped his gaze to his open geography book and made no sign. So William got the kitten Pauline had named Tiger.

Back from the village that afternoon, the teacher scooped Jibby up into his arms and, holding her against his chest, stroked her again and again. She tolerated his gentle touch, but she neither purred nor rubbed her head under his chin as she used to. Victor wondered if she had sensed his censure. Cats, he re-flected, always returned like for like. Perhaps she had felt neglected. Now she, too, would neglect her master.

Victor shrugged his shoulders, set the cat down on the floor, and gave her haunches a parting pat. Jibby raised her tail high and went back to her mouse-watch outside Pauline's pantry.

As the days went by, Jibby took to lurking around outside. Soon she was joined by three toms, who sur-rounded her, yowling and screeching. The dreadful song fest seemed to afford a malicious pleasure to them all. But soon the tomcats became morose, turned furious, and fell upon each other like wild devils. Calm in spirit and enjoying it all, Jibby watched the battle.

Pauline's patience snapped. She poured a pail of

water out of the window over the unseemly company and put an end to the show.

"Tasso," she called, "find the cat."

The tomcats broke away from each other and scattered in the general direction of Julius' barn. Jibby fled indoors. Tasso briefly wagged his stump of a tail and spread his mouth wide in a look that seemed to promise a bark—or a yawn. Instead he pranced forward shaking his head and acting like a merry teddy bear.

"Peep," said the canary and launched into his best trills and cadenzas.

"He's my favorite among your animals," Pauline stated grimly to Victor, amused at her own annoyance. "At least he really sings and he never makes a fuss."

After that the house and yard could not hold Jibby: she began to roam. For half, sometimes whole, days nobody knew where she was. Actually she crouched in the fields and stalked mice—not disdaining very large grasshoppers or frogs.

Time and again Victor went out in front of the house and called: "Jibby. Here, Jibby!"

"Let her be," Pauline advised. "When she wants something to eat, she'll come by herself."

But the schoolmaster missed Jibby. He had taken her in, out of the cold, off the open road; and for her part Jibby had trusted him out of the whole world and asked for his protection. He wished she would come in and rub against his leg. He wanted to stroke her soft fur and make her purr. He missed the soundless music of her movements in his workaday study.

Victor not only felt deserted; he worried about Jibby. He knew cats didn't "go wild"—a cat never ceases to be a wild animal in the first place. She only has her tame, her charming, hours. The cat is the only beast of prey who has learned how to make humankind provide her with food and shelter. All his principles to the contrary, Victor feared that Jibby would not come home again.

Jibby had started out early that day and trailed a hare far out along the road until she saw a strange boy lumbering toward her from the direction of the village. He stooped and held out his long arms. But Jibby dived off the side of the road after her hare and forgot the boy entirely.

While Jibby hunted the hare, the boy hunted Jibby.

William, the locksmith's son, was about twelve years old, big for his years, strong and scowling-faced. His brown hair grew so close to his eyes that he had hardly any forehead. He sneaked up on the cat from behind. His left hand clutched a length of hard twine, and his right hand held a pair of his father's pliers.

Jibby stopped in her tracks and got ready to pounce on her prey. William pinched her tail with the pliers and looped a lasso around her neck. When the boy stood up and the cat pulled away, the string pinched her throat.

William looked around him until he spied an oak sapling by the fence—just the thing for his favorite game. He threw the end of his string over a low limb and began hauling Jibby up off the ground. Up and up she went, when Tasso came crashing through the field, baring his sharp teeth at the boy.

Now, though William loved to tease little cats, he was afraid of big dogs. He dropped the string and ran off down the road toward the village. Behind him, at the side of the road, Tasso bit through the loop of twine about Jibby's neck, took her body up in his powerful jaws, and trotted off for home.

Tasso ran into the house, carrying Jibby in his mouth. She hung limp without moving a muscle, folded over between his jaws. Panic filled Victor. Could Tasso have hurt Jibby?

Pauline must have had the same fear.

"Tasso!" she called in loud alarm.

At her cry Tasso put Jibby lightly on the floor; and the cat, tail held high, scooted around the dog's legs.

Boys like William have single-track minds and very poor judgment. Two days later William slipped into the schoolmaster's yard and lay flat on his belly behind the well house, planning to waylay the cat and twist her tail. Inside the house, Tasso's prolonged growl drew Pauline out of the kitchen to the front door. Just in time to hear Jibby screech, she saw the boy reaching with his pliers for Jibby's tail. Pauline rushed out and grabbed him by his hair. She shook him back and forth and gave him a loud slap.

"What's going on?" Victor asked, walking up the path toward them. The boy stood with bowed head and sullen face.

"He's a bad boy," Pauline stormed. "Torturing animals! I'll give him what he deserves." She tightened her grasp on his hair and yanked his head around to face his teacher.

"So— You torture animals?" Victor said softly. He was trembling with rage and hatred. William kept his glance fixed on the ground and remained silent. Victor forced himself to cross the yard slowly

[105]

and lay a hand on the boy's stubborn shoulder. "Where is your own kitten?" he asked sternly. He looked from the boy to the pliers Pauline was snatching up from the grass by the well. From the pliers his gaze traveled back to the boy. "What happened to the cat I gave you last week?"

Pauline gave an angry gasp, and they heard her skirt rustle as she ran across the grass to the porch step, where she stood with her back to them, listening.

William cringed.

"You heard me," Victor went on, still gripping the boy's shoulder. "Where is he?"

"It ran away," said William, giving the man a sly look of triumph.

"So much the worse for you, my boy. That serves you right. You have your work cut out for you. Find the kitten, and you may come to school tomorrow. Tell your father that, when he asks—"

William started to cry.

"And tell him," Victor went on, "you cannot come to school at all without the kitten you were supposed to take care of. Now hurry. I'll return these myself," he added, taking the pliers from Pauline's hand and dropping them in his jacket pocket, "and warn your father to watch his tools after this."

"But it's lost, I tell you," William blubbered. "It ran away. Really it did."

"All right. That will teach you that animals—even little kittens—are not weak and defenseless. See how the kitten has punished you? You cannot come to school. Your father will learn the reason. The whole village will know about you. And listen to Tasso! No one has to sic him on you. I shall have to hold him to keep him from chasing you all the way back to the village."

He took his hand off the boy's arm, turned quickly, and caught Tasso just as the dog sprang at the boy.

"Run!" he called, holding the big dog by his powerful shoulders and hugging him close against his own body. "Run for your life!"

CHAPTER VII

VISITORS

OUT INTO THE WORLD spread the rumor of Victor and Pauline's hospitality. Out over the animal grapevine went the wonderful story of Jibby, the cat that had a charming, noble hunting dog for a knight errant. And into the teacher's house came a steady stream of visitors from afar.

First to arrive was a stately Persian tomcat. He slipped quietly in the front door one morning. He wandered around the spacious study leisurely inspecting every corner and sat down next to Jibby on the sofa. Jibby received her strange guest with dignity and a distant kind of friendliness.

When Victor and Pauline said hello, the tomcat displayed good manners, purring when stroked. But he made it clear that he did not want to stir from Jibby's side.

"Well, then, stay there," Victor told him.

"But you be nice when Tasso comes in," Pauline cautioned. "He won't hurt you. Besides, we allow no fighting in this house."

The Persian gazed at her intently.

"A big cat like that has a lot of strength," Pauline went on, "and a lot of temperament too. You can't tell what he'll start."

"If he is treated well, he will behave well," Victor said, crossing over to the tom. "What shall we call you?" he asked. "Rustan?"

At the name the Persian looked up, pointing his ears. He stared quizzically into the teacher's face.

"You've guessed his name," Pauline laughed. "Or something close to it."

The Persian stood up, arched his back, and spat. Tasso was coming in, flanks heaving from his morning run in the pasture behind the house. In his amazement he came forward slowly and carefully. The tom sat down again and awaited the dog, though with obvious nervousness.

The two animals gazed at each other a long time. Then Tasso romped away and came back. He seemed to be laughing. It could not be said that Tasso won over the Persian once and forever. But it looked as if the visiting cat was going to tolerate Tasso's friendliness.

"Well, then," said Victor with some satisfaction, "there'll be no fight. They're going to get along."

"Let's hope so." Pauline was skeptical.

"Good Tasso. Good Rustan." The teacher stepped between them and stroked both the dog and the Persian. "If you could only tell us where you came from, and why you've come."

The Persian listened hard. Tasso made believe that he understood everything. He lifted a forepaw onto the sofa edge to lend emphasis to his master's words.

Jibby stretched out on her side and the Persian did the same. He patted her neck with his paw, and Jibby acknowledged the attention by mewing softly and happily.

"It's obvious why he has come," Pauline laughed. "Just look at Jibby!"

However, Rustan stayed with Jibby only a few days. Another tomcat came to call: an ordinary fellow with a scarred black pelt and torn ears that told of many a wild battle.

"He's no good," Victor said.

"Poor devil," said Pauline, taking pity on the shabby tom. "The things he must have been through!"

"Only because he's quarrelsome."

Victor was right. The shabby tom wasted no time before he attacked the Persian. The Persian evaded the attack, retreating on delicate feet to the ledge along the high sofa back. When Shabby Tom, pressing his advantage, still threatened him, Rustan fled through the window into the open and ran for the field across the road.

"We'll never see him again," said Pauline, looking after him.

"Coward," grumbled Victor.

But the triumph of Shabby Tom, toward whom Jibby took a tender attitude, was short-lived. Victor and Pauline let him stay, although they did not love him either; but his rude ways provoked Tasso. In the beginning the otter hound was merely surprised by Shabby Tom's bad manners. Soon, however, he got so angry that he grabbed the tom violently, swung him through the air, and hurled him against the wall.

The tomcat was stunned. He lay silent where he had fallen. Tasso rushed at him.

"Tasso!" Victor shouted. "What are you doing?"

In the middle of a spring the dog halted, ears swinging. Wagging his tail, he paced over to his master and looked questioningly and softly into his eyes.

"Don't be a murderer," Victor warned him.

"That's right, Tasso," said Pauline. "No need to kill him."

The dog looked from man to wife, from wife to man, and back at the disgraceful Shabby Tom. He lifted his lips and revealed his terrible teeth.

"Enough, my good fellow," Victor said mildly. "You've punished him. That's enough."

"Yes, Tasso. You are good," Pauline praised him.

Ready for peace the dog wagged his tail and sat down near the prostrate cat, watching him closely. When Shabby Tom sat up, Tasso gave a growling, rising bark. Shabby Tom arose, sneaked timidly past the growling dog, climbed on the sofa, edged up close to Jibby, and sat down.

Jibby put forth all her arts of coquetry and seductiveness. Shabby Tom was too dull or too boorish to respond. Jibby sat up in a pet and looked away from her surly suitor. But, once the teacher picked her up, she purred and climbed his shoulder.

The tomcat spat.

"Careful," Pauline said.

"What for? No animal has ever hurt me."

"There's always a first time."

The tomcat leaped from the sofa and rushed at Victor's legs with distended jaws and bared claws. Tasso sprang between them and the tom ducked away, snarling.

A day or two later a little dog wandered into the yard, and Tasso brought him in. He was young, masterless, of no known breed, playful—and starved. His loneliness and desire to serve Man—showing stronger than his expectation of being fed—caught their hearts. He leaped comically upon Tasso, snapping playfully at his ears and flanks and Tasso took it all like a good-natured uncle.

Then the little dog spied Jibby and Shabby Tom, and began to curse. No doubt about it, he was cursing; his voice sounded different from the tone he used with Tasso. It was hostile, even threatening—in a comical way. He made a great deal of noise, and still Jibby ignored him. But Shabby Tom arched his back, cursed back, and hit out at the little dog with his paws.

[113]

"Now what?" Victor asked.

The little dog stopped his racket. He rolled over on his back and lay in the middle of the floor offering devoted, unconditional obedience. His tail—his whole body—wagged the news that he was without a will of his own.

"What a funny fellow!" Pauline, bending down over him, was touched. "And so young and thin, Victor."

"Hardly more than a puppy."

"A noisy child and an amusing one. Shall we keep him?"

"You know we never chase any animal away, Pauline."

"I don't want to chase the little ragamuffin away."

Victor snapped his fingers.

"You've already found the right name for him," he said. "Let's call him Rags."

"Well, my little Rags, I'll bring you something— something better than a name." Pauline brought from the kitchen a feeding dish filled to the brim. "Rags, you are invited to have dinner with Tasso."

Tasso ate a few mouthfuls, while Rags sat with cocked head and pointed ears, whimpering softly, trembling with covetousness. Tasso raised his head, wagged his curl of tail, and stepped aside.

"Come on, Rags." Pauline encouraged the newcomer. "It all belongs to you now." She watched Rags dip his muzzle into the big dish. "He'll never be able to force that much down," she whispered.

But Rags could indeed manage everything in the big feeding dish. Crazily he devoured it—*hap, hap, hap!*—gulping as if he had never known what it meant to have a full meal. In a flash all the food vanished—more than enough to satisfy the giant Tasso. Rags sank to the floor, his belly full and round. He heaved a deep sigh and fell asleep.

Jibby disdained Rags like a queen. She lay on the sofa with Shabby Tom while the little dog was prancing around and around. Meanwhile Tasso lay stretched out full length on the floor before the fireplace. He cocked his ears as Rags danced around the two cats.

Rags circled the sofa once more, giving vent to a string of short, friendly barks; then, with the speed of a released arrow, he circled the room. Shabby Tom sat up and reached out an angry paw toward the little dog. Back Rags came again and repeated the game, unmindful of the tomcat's threats.

"Watch it, Tasso," Victor addressed the big dog in a low tone.

All at once Rag's barks of pure joy broke into a piercing cry of pain. He had a bloody scratch over his eye. Above him Shabby Tom stood with his paw still outstretched. Rags whimpered and crawled away, slipping through the door into the kitchen. The next instant Pauline appeared in the doorway with Rags in one arm.

"This is too awful," she scolded. Holding Rags up, she inspected the bleeding wound and tried to soothe the little fellow.

Tasso had risen to his feet. His growl rumbled like thunder. Jibby leaped down off the sofa and climbed into Victor's chair.

"She knows who her friend is," said Pauline sternly. "She knows Shabby Tom's going to be punished."

Shabby Tom found himself alone facing the big, angry dog. He spat and slapped the air with a tentative paw.

Tasso gave tongue to his fury. His rolling growl rose into a high-pitched, hate-filled rattling and ear-splitting, nerve-wracking bay. Then his powerful jaws snapped shut on the back of the flinching tomcat. The tomcat yowled, and Tasso strode to the door with him.

"Good dog," Pauline said.

"Easy, Tasso!" Victor commanded.

"Go on, Tasso," Pauline cried. "Break the devil's neck."

Out in the front yard, Shabby Tom hung half-conscious in Tasso's jaws. The dog shook him so violently that it seemed the tom could not live. The dog hurled him to the ground and sniffed the limp form. The tom stirred; and Tasso picked him up, shook him like a rag, and again cast him on the grass. Then he cocked his head, looking down at the cat and wagging his tail.

"Enough, Tasso!" Pauline called, stepping out of the door.

"He didn't kill him!" Victor was at her side, holding Jibby. "He made him a gift of his life. Good dog."

Gaily but making no boasts, Tasso came up to his master. He gratefully accepted their praises and pats on the back. Rags pranced happily around, his wound already forgotten.

All the fight had been knocked out of the tomcat. Dizzily he wavered to his feet with the plain intention of sneaking back into the house. Tasso barred his way. The big dog barked angrily, and tiny Rags seconded him industriously. It was too much for the battered tom. He turned tail and weaved across the yard toward the road.

Tasso barked thunderously. Shabby Tom ran faster. Tasso chased him through the gate and there took up his post, going into a fury each time the cat tried to slink back past him. At last the tom crossed the road and disappeared over the field. For a while longer Tasso held his watch by the gate, with Rags boldly doing sentry duty near by.

One morning at breakfast another visitor came bounding in. The new tomcat was a very young fellow with a gray coat like Jibby's liberally striped in black. He was full of droll mannerisms. He roamed the room in darts and leaps. He hid his head under the hem of Pauline's skirt. Under Jibby's haughty stare, he chased his tail. Obviously and instantaneously enchanted, Jibby romped affectionately with him.

It looked like a match.

"Ladies and gentlemen," declaimed Pauline, tapping the stove top with a spoon. "Is it all right with everybody if I call him Tige?"

Tige had come to stay. He won the early approval of Tasso, who rolled him on the floor with due care—

a game that Tige joined in the proper spirit. He was a born tumbler.

Rags, too, loved him with all the good humor of his youth. For one thing, the newcomer did not always hunch on the sofa with Jibby. On the contrary, he jumped down to play with Rags as often as the little dog invited him. Then the two of them rolled across the floor embracing each other. This sport went so well that Jibby refused to remain a lonely onlooker. She slipped down from her throne, joined in the glad camaraderie, and was soon reigning over the game.

"Hello!" Julius said from the doorway. "This looks pretty gay."

"This is how we like it," said Pauline, making a great show of picking her way over the floor among the whirling animals in her path.

Rags, the little clown, danced around the visitor, wagging his tail passionately. He took the taciturn farmer by surprise.

"You're a cute little dog!" Amazed at himself, Julius clumsily patted Rags, who lay on his back before him in a attitude of complete devotion.

Presently Jibby ran out of the house and roamed restlessly around the yard. She ran out into the road, young Tige and Rags happily prancing after. Then, before they knew it, she was off through the fields, leaving them behind. She repeated this trick day after day.

"Where's Jibby, Pauline?" the teacher asked anxiously one day when he returned to an empty study. "I don't like this wandering the fields so much."

"Nothing can happen to her. She's hunting for mice, and I don't have any here. Tige and Rags are out with her."

"You can hardly call those two protectors."

"Jibby protects herself, Victor."

And so it proved. The next day, for once, Jibby stayed home. Suddenly a rat went speeding across the yard, so big and fat it looked as if it were stuffed. Rags saw it first. He circled around it wildly, blocking its path.

Jibby shot out of the house. For a moment she crouched, her head jerking right and left to follow the zigzag progress of the rat. Slipping across the grass, lurking behind him, creeping closer, she looked like a magnificent lion. Then she executed a well-aimed dash.

Drawn by Rags's mad barking, Victor came to the door. Jibby had struck the rat and pulled back to see how much damage she had done. The rat was quaking and whistling with fear. Before it could whistle again, Jibby had it by the neck and she held on until its spine broke in two. She shook the thick body and hastily dropped it, turning away in disgust. Her measured step had great dignity. She paced away from the scene in the manner of one who had performed a righteous act of justice. By her side tumbled Rags and Tige.

Jibby had something important to do. She avoided Victor who was ready to stroke and praise her. She sprang up on the bench beside the door and began carefully to wash herself. Fetching a flat shovel, the schoolmaster scooped up the body of the dead rat and laid it out of sight in the shade of the privet hedge. Later on he would bury it in the pasture.

Her toilette made, Jibby ran out on the road, escorted by Rags and Tige.

"Tasso," Pauline called from the front door. "Quick! Fetch the cat."

The otter hound loped off and presently came back carrying Jibby. Limp and dead-looking, she dangled from his mouth. Tige and Rags brought up the rear in the manner of a funeral cortege.

"Tasso!" exclaimed Victor in alarm.

Looking up from under his humorous blond eyebrows, the dog put the cat on the grass before his master. Jibby spryly got to her feet and paced back and forth in the space between Tasso's forelegs, her tail lifted so that it impudently swiped the big dog's face.

"Well!" Pauline was delighted. "That's the way it should be. Back to your old tricks!"

After supper Victor took their chairs into the front yard and set them together between the bird bath and the well. He and Pauline sat there, enjoying the evening in the white light of the moon. Indoors Jibby, Tige, and Rags were fast asleep, lying together on the sofa. Tasso was staying up with his people. He stretched out across their feet.

The stillness almost sang. Around them the fields lay like folds of black velvet, and overhead the wide sky was illuminated by a bright full moon.

"It's like an enchantment," Pauline said quietly. "And there's something happy and something sad about it." Of this odd couple the man was ordinarily the dreamer and idealist; the woman the cool and practical one. She stirred, shivering a little in the tweed jacket she had draped over her shoulders. She leaned closer to her husband.

"That rat," she whispered. "Victor, why are we so hard on rats?"

"Why not? There are animals that are alien and hostile to man, just as there are animals on man's side. There are quiet animals that serve man—like the ox. They could love us if we gave them the love that is imagination. Pigs too. Pigs are very charming." Victor laid his hand over Pauline's. He was referring, she knew, to her ambition to raise pigs some day.

"But rats?" he went on. "Let me see. Well, maybe a rat could strike up a kind of friendship with a solitary prisoner in a jail—an ancient, moldy dungeon."

"Ugh!" grunted Pauline, and they both laughed.

"Take the spider." Victor said. "Most people have a horror of spiders. They can't imagine how wise they are or that they could be tame. Snakes too, if they're not poisonous. Now I remember! Once I read about a young man who brought home an adder. He told his father he had bought it in a pet shop. Why? the father asked him. Was it the only thing the man had to sell? The snake had looked lonely, the son explained. Customers gathered around the puppies and the parrots, while no one came to admire the adder. The young man kept the adder in his bedroom and waited for a chance to set it free in the country—in the mountains.

"One day a friend of his father's came to lunch and

[123]

somehow the adder in the house was mentioned. The guest asked to see it, and the young man brought it down from his room and put it on the table. For a while it lay still and then it began to crawl around, searching here and there. The guest—not a timid man, apparently—reached out his hand to it. The adder made as if to strike at it with its tongue, hesitated, and turned away as if it had made up its mind about something. It also turned away from the father's hand. But it knew the hand of the youth. It ran up its master's arm to his shoulder, coiled there, and laid its beautiful head gently on the man's head. The snake was contented, I think. Fear—and the instinct of self-preservation that fear calls into play—was suspended."

"If it could happen to a snake," Pauline mused, "why isn't it true of all animals? And certainly boys have pet turtles and lizards— Maybe it is true—if we knew the way."

"I have a theory—" Victor hesitated.

"Go ahead."

"We human beings were banished from the Garden of Eden," he said. "But among some of us there are leftover instincts—fragments of the peace and innocence we had in full measure back in the Garden.

One of these, perhaps, makes us desire to be comrades with the animals. And instinct knows a way, or it wouldn't be an instinct. So we are equipped already with a means of communication with animals, fragmentary as it is." Victor paused and sighed.

"What can come of it?" Energetically Pauline broke off the discussion. "After all, we should try to change things that lie within our power to change. Don't be a blind explorer in the animal dark."

"Really, Pauline?" the schoolmaster said. "But suppose I do apply myself to human problems only. Do we understand each other so well? Tell me truly, is the cat-sense or dog-sense I use on Jibby or Tasso such a waste of time? Suppose it helps me to see the children at their desks or Julius or—you?"

"Victor," Pauline said, stretching out her hand to him in the moon-drenched garden, "it does help."

The man, woman, and dog rose and slowly walked to the house together.

CHAPTER VIII

TROUBLE

ONCE AGAIN a company of rival tomcats screeched, sobbed, and sang outside in the dark. Tige, the young tom, full of battle fever, got up to go out and join them. But Jibby lifted a paw and he bowed to her will. It was evident that these two had mated.

Instead, Tasso sneaked out into the yard, Rags trotting after him; and the two brought the unearthly serenade to a quick end. All Tasso had to do was put in an appearance. For his part Rags jumped up and down so fast that he gave the effect of two dogs. His falsetto yapping created a sensation. Finally he chased and harried the routed tomcats into the shadow of the barn down the road.

In these days Jibby's deportment turned gentle and her manner tender. It delighted Victor that she could never get enough of his petting.

"Why, Victor!" exclaimed Pauline, holding the purring Jibby in her arms and feeling her body. "Kitty is with litter."

For yet a little while, in spite of her condition, Jibby kept running out into the fields. She swaggered up and down the road as if she owned it, and she stalked endless mice. Two or three times a week Tasso brought her home.

When her time drew near, she no longer went out. She paced the room restlessly and threw a pleading glance now at Victor, now at Pauline. As for young Tige and gay little Rags, she waved them away. She allowed Tasso alone to be near her.

One day she followed Pauline all over the house, plaintively and impatiently mewing with each step they took. Something was wrong. Pauline bent down and laid a hand on her head. Jibby pressed her brow to the hand, gave out a loud cry, and bore a kitten.

Victor picked up mother and child, and carried them to the lying-in bed he had made up again and installed in the old corner.

But it was the only kitten Jibby was carrying, and she spent the riches of her motherly care on her single baby. She cleaned, licked, and guarded the blind and motionless little bundle. It would not suckle. Time and again Jibby laid the little creature, which had arrived in this world only to leave it, against her breast. She made countless attempts to stroke and warm it into life—licking, licking, licking—but in an hour it was dead. Still Jibby did not give up.

Victor gently lifted the mother to his chest and crooned words of comfort over her, while Pauline gathered up the dead child. Jibby fought to get away from him so Victor let her go and she went looking for her little one. She wandered over the entire house, whining to herself in a high thin mew. Outside Pauline was busy with a spade in the cemetery at the corner of the fence.

The rest of the household stayed remarkably quiet. Young Tige did not move a limb. He cowered timidly on the sofa while Jibby made the rounds, softly calling for her lost kitten. She went up to Tasso and gazed into his face, beseeching him. Then she turned to Victor and to Pauline, and mutely asked the same thing of them.

"We should have let her watch you bury it," said Victor, anger edging his voice.

"Cats have short memories." Pauline shrugged her shoulders. "She'll forget it soon."

But it seemed to Victor that for a long time Jibby did not forget. She gave up the search but she still meowed in her dismal way, apparently hoping Victor or Pauline would return her child to her. When no one brought her a kitten, she looked dignified and distant. It was days before they could get her to purr.

Young Tige, Jibby, and Rags were playing together in the yard: it was like old times. Then they scattered as a big rat rushed by, making tracks for his nest under the porch steps. Young Tige who was hardly as long and by no means as heavy as the rat, sprang. And indeed the rat turned upon him to defend itself and bit him hard right in the shoulder.

Tige recoiled with an astonished yowl of pain.

At once Jibby caught the ugly animal with one practiced grab at the neck, bit through its spine before it could even whistle, and flung it into the flower bed.

Brave young Tige was bleeding from shoulder to forepaw. Meowing with pain and horror, he slunk into the kitchen. He hid in a corner and began licking his wound. But the next day the wound showed no sign of healing.

Victor coaxed Tige to let him examine it.

"A rat bite can be poisonous," he said.

Tige went on for several days, licking the wound that refused to heal. And slowly he lost his gaiety. When Jibby invited him to play, he lifted a paw and let it drop weakly. Next day he stopped washing himself, and his fur became scraggly and lost its luster. Jibby began to avoid him—apparently to fear him a little.

"Pauline, look at the little fellow."

"Why don't we send to town for the vet?"

The veterinary was a young, good-humored man whom they both liked.

"Who's sick, Victor?" he asked as soon as he stepped in the door. "Not Tasso!"

It was hard to catch the ailing Tige. He ducked and weakly evaded the reaching hands, but they cornered him at last. Captured in the firm hands of the vet, he tried to scratch and bite. But the young man held him so expertly that he soon calmed down enough to be examined.

"There isn't a lot I can do," pronounced the vet, shrugging his shoulders. "He's poisoned. He may throw it off, but I doubt he can. Do you want me to give him a lethal hypodermic? It will stop the pain right away. And it takes just a second to work. There's no extra suffering, I promise you."

"Yes!" cried Pauline.

"No!" Victor was saying at the same time just as positively. "Do you think he might be able to overcome the poison?" he added.

"I think he might. But only 'might.' "

Pauline walked away.

"We'll take a chance on it."

After the young man had gone, Tige went back to licking his wound, but only briefly. Another day passed and he vanished. They went over the whole house looking for him. Jibby kept to herself on the sofa. Again they called Tasso to help.

"Where is Tige?" Victor asked. "Fetch Tige."

The dog sniffed busily all over the study. He rooted in all the corners of the kitchen and in the cupboards and the pantry. Back in the teacher's study, he poked his nose under the furniture. When he came to the sofa, he drew back sharply in fear. In one flying leap Jibby sailed across the room halfway to the kitchen door.

"That's where he is!"

"And not alive any more," Pauline said sadly.

"How do you know?" Victor asked from the floor where he was down on his knees feeling under the sofa as far as he could reach.

"Didn't you see how frightened they got?" Pauline replied. "That's a sure sign."

They moved the sofa and back against the wall the little tomcat lay stretched out. He had crawled away to die alone.

Pauline's eyes filled with tears. Victor felt a quick relief. The rat bite was open and swollen and in-flamed. They buried the thin, pathetic body in the fence-corner.

The population of the animal graveyard under the apple tree was growing fast. Victor counted the little mounds. First of all, there was the dove Jibby had hunted to its death. Next to the dove lay Jibby's lion-colored daughter whom the terrier had struck down. The newest grave, third in the original row, was still fresh—the grave Pauline had dug for the still-born kitten.

Into a new grave, larger than the others, Victor lowered Tige. He had dug it so that the young father could rest beside the one child he had sired. The teacher went into the kitchen and got out the jar of round white pebbles he kept there for his sling shot. He outlined the fresh grave with a border of little stones that gleamed in the grass of the plot. Then he did the same for the other three little mounds.

Victor was just getting up from this sentimental labor when a small truck came roaring and thumping up. As it drew abreast of the graveyard, it clattered to a stop. At the steering wheel sat Julius.

"Well, are you surprised?" Julius called out. "I got it cheap. Now I can take my corn and cane to town faster and make more money. By next year the thing'll be paid for."

"Pretty fancy," Victor shouted above the chug of the engine.

"Guess what." Julius cut out the engine. "I've just stocked something pretty good."

"Hogs?"

"I have hogs."

"Turkeys?"

"I've had turkeys since last fall."

"All right, Julius, what?"

[133]

"Something that increases fast, needs no care, and tastes as good as chicken!"

"Ah! Rabbits."

"You guessed it." Julius beamed. "Twenty of them. Bought them very cheap. We've already killed a few and they're mighty fine eating. And we still have as many as before."

"Good luck!" called Victor across the fence.

"Thanks!" Julius started the engine again. After long and continued coughing it finally started to run. "It will spare the horses," he shouted, but the thunder of the truck swallowed his voice. He waved and rolled away.

"Julius is going to be rich," the teacher declared.

"Have you noticed Rags?" Pauline asked from the front door, where she was waiting for Victor to return from work. A few weeks had gone by without incident.

"Rags?" Victor exclaimed. "What about Rags?"

"Since yesterday. He's very subdued."

Hansi the canary suddenly sang out in a loud burst of trills, putting courage and good humor into Victor.

"Oh," he said absent-mindedly.

[134]

"He ambles so," persisted Pauline. "His hind quarters look as if they've come unhinged from the rest of him. And he hasn't touched a bite all day."

"Stomach ache. That happens to dogs occasionally."

"Tasso never gets anything like that," Pauline insisted.

"Oh, him!" The teacher said proudly. "He's a hero. Just as soon imagine Hercules with indigestion."

"Take a look at Rags."

The little clown was very sick indeed. The next morning he did not get up. He lay still on his side, his eyes glassy, his nose dry and hot.

"Distemper!" Victor pronounced.

Jibby deserted. She refused to stay next to Rags on the sofa. She abandoned this friend as she had abandoned young Tige. Rags gave one weak wag of his tail as a sign of devotion. Then he lost consciousness.

The cheerful vet with the clever hands confirmed Victor's diagnosis. He pulled an ugly-looking injection needle out of his satchel. Victor kept silent. Rags's body shuddered and his hind legs stiffened.

"Paralysis setting in," said the vet. "The beginning of the end."

"Put him out of his misery, Doctor," Pauline said energetically.

The veterinary plunged the needle into Rags's breast. The little dog did not even flinch. All Victor could think of was Rags's gay barking.

CHAPTER IX

PRINCESS FROM FAR AWAY

O NE FINE SUMMER AFTERNOON a magnificent white angora walked into the house. She was humble yet confident, sly but very proud. Sparkling white, long-haired, she enchanted Victor and Pauline.

Wednesday and Thursday she stayed only a few hours and fled the moment Jibby came home. But Jibby took no notice of her. Friday the snow-white cat simply stayed all night. She had made it plain that she wished to make this her home.

"Where could she have come from?" Victor wondered. "No one around here has such a fine animal."

"Oh, you know cats," Pauline said, "and you know

[137]

how stupid some people are. No doubt somewhere they treated her badly."

"She's beautiful!"

"Magnificent," Pauline agreed. "Come here! Come here, you beauty!" To their amazement, the angora leaped in a graceful arc right into Pauline's arms, catching her claws in the rough tweed of her jacket. Pauline embraced the cat, and the animal relaxed gently and flatteringly, pushing closer to the woman, whipping her gorgeous bushy tail back and forth.

"Smooth and soft as silk," Pauline declared admiringly. She stroked the cat on her breast. "Call her, Victor. Maybe she'll go to you too."

He was standing some four paces away.

"Kitty! White kitty!" he called softly.

The angora pointed her ears and lifted her shoulder. Her big eyes, the pupils like small, dark lashes, looked around the room. Her face wore a pensive expression as if she were trying to decide something. Then with a single leap she flew to the man's shoulder. He reached out a hand to steady her, but she slipped to the other shoulder. He felt her sharp claws through his shirt. Trembling with the effort of balancing, she crouched tight and leaned against his neck and cheek. Her tail beat powerfully on his back.

Then she began to purr—so loud, so high-pitched
and joyous, so bright and compelling, that Victor and
Pauline broke into laughter. It seemed to heighten
the angora's good mood, and she purred louder and
higher.

Hansi took up the challenge and began to twitter.
After a moment the angora slipped to the floor in
another of her great arcs and marched around the
room as if she wished to acquaint herself with her
new quarters. She was wholly at ease. She peered into
all the corners and looked over every possible sitting
place. When Pauline offered her a dish of milk, she
walked up to it with ceremony. In all graciousness she
appeared to be making her own decisions. She let
nothing shake her composure.

Tasso came into the room, wagging his tail.

The angora did not even arch her back. Instead she
ran to meet the dog. He sniffed at her, still wagging
his tail. She sat up on her hindquarters and embraced
him, her forelegs wrapped around his lowered head.
It was both touching and ridiculous. After a while
the angora dropped her forepaws back on the floor
and retreated a few steps.

"Now she'll attack," Victor whispered. But there
was no attack.

[139]

The cat and the big dog looked at each other. The angora purred briefly and Tasso licked her muzzle. The angora turned away from him and back to her milk dish. Slowly she sat down before it and drank a little more. Tasso watched near by. Every line of his body seemed to encourage the angora to enjoy herself with the milk.

Suddenly she tensed, turned away from the saucer, and pointed her delicate ears. Jibby leaped in through the window and stormed at the angora.

How it happened neither Victor nor Pauline could say afterward. The angora, so far as they could see, did not lift a paw; yet she must have pushed Jibby away with a mighty blow, for Jibby was thrown against the wall. Obviously shaken, she pulled herself together and sat mewing—all the fight gone out of her.

"No, Jibby." Victor picked her up. "I won't let the fine lady manhandle you. You're my good old girl. Right?"

Jibby did not purr. Nor did she rub her head under his chin as he went on stroking her. She lay still on his chest, opening her jaws now and then for a plaintive, almost soundless meow.

"There's something the matter with her." Victor scratched Jibby gently.

"There's nothing the matter with her," Pauline said. "She's insulted and jealous, that's all."

"Jibby, be nice now," Victor coaxed. "There's no reason for you to be jealous. The white lady is bigger and stronger than you are, but she won't touch you any more. You're my favorite."

But Jibby would not be comforted. The teacher held her for a long time, but he could not get her to make a single one of her old friendly responses. On the contrary, she tried to get away from him. He had to let her have her way, and she slipped to the floor. She ran away from him indifferently; and, the first chance she got, she was out the door.

From then on the angora lived in the house unmolested. There was not the slightest friction between the two cats. Jibby and White Lady drank their cream out of the same dish. Between Jibby and Tasso it was like old times. She slept on his bed and tyrannized over him as always. The angora slept elegantly and alone in one corner of the sofa. She made no hostile approaches to the canary bird and wandered around the yard among the doves and chickens without seeming to be aware of their existence.

With Tasso she developed a polite relationship, and it evidently did not occur to her to try to lord it over him the way Jibby did.

"The angora's a pleasant house companion, isn't she?" Pauline remarked at the evening meal. "And Hansi. Neither of them makes any trouble."

"Better than that. The bird delights with his singing, and the white lady with her beauty."

"And nobility," Pauline added.

Tasso's unshakable love, however, belonged to Jibby. The big dog's devotion helped Jibby endure the angora. She counted on Tasso's standing by in an emergency—a specific emergency at that.

Now Jibby ran off to the mouse-hunt in the fields more often than ever. In a stubborn mood no one understood, she developed a penchant for sitting in the middle of the road. And when she deigned to come in, she paid no attention to Victor. Two nights in a row she shied away from him, almost as if she were guilty of some misdeed. One afternoon she lapped up only a little of the dish of cream Pauline set out for her. Victor tried to get her to come to him, but she simply ignored him. Her manner was strange, almost hostile.

Toward evening Jibby darted out into the garden,

then under the fence to the other side of the road. Victor, standing in the front yard, could see a giant Persian cat poised on the crest of a slight ridge that marked the edge of the field across the way. Jibby sat down beside him, whereupon the Persian raised a terrific racket. Pauline wanted to chase him away.

"No," Victor laughed. "He's paying court to our Jibby."

The Persian Tom continued to yowl.

"I don't know how long I can stand this—even for your sake," Pauline called above the clamor. Without another word she ran down the yard. She picked up a pail of water that she kept near the gate for her flowers, and hurled its contents toward the enamoured cats. Lots of women are good marksmen with a bucket. The cascade caught the cats squarely, and the noise stopped the same instant. Like a streak of lightning the Persian vanished behind the rise of ground. Jibby darted back across the road, in the gate past Pauline, and through the study door.

In two seconds Jibby appeared in the doorway, looking as casual as if she had no objective. Then, in a lingering kind of walk, she strolled icily past them and out the gate again.

"We've driven her away," said Victor.

"Gone to look for her lover," Pauline scoffed.

Neither was right. But they were soon to find out Jibby's secret.

One day Julius stomped into the house, angry and excited.

"Some animal is stealing my rabbits," he announced. A second or two of silence passed.

"Really?" said Victor at last.

"One a day!" The farmer pounded on the desk with his fist.

"Maybe it's a fox," Pauline suggested.

"Marten, more likely," Victor said.

"A marten, a marten," Julius laughed scornfully. "In this house of all houses you ought to know better. A marten would kill all the rabbits at once."

"Fence in your rabbit hutches so nothing can get in," Pauline suggested. "Neither a fox nor a marten."

"You know as much about these things, Pauline," the farmer said with elaborate sarcasm, "as a cow that tries to slip through a fence."

Pauline laughed and nodded.

"Suppose it's a fox," Julius went on. "Can you imagine a fox that comes back night after night and every time takes only a single rabbit?"

"Hardly possible," Victor said gravely.

"This beast is very sly," Julius grumbled.

"Slyer than you are, at any rate," Pauline murmured.

"Let me catch that animal," said Julius, ignoring Pauline, "and I'll kill it on the spot."

"Of course," Pauline said in a tone of finality.

Jibby slunk by the farmer and scooted outside. Tasso followed her, and, as he passed Julius in his turn, he growled. Victor looked at his friend with sharp distrust.

"Why is the dog growling?" he demanded. "That's not his manner."

"I never did anything to Tasso," Julius said.

"It's strange anyway," Victor said.

"Ah! And who is this?" Julius exclaimed suddenly. He moved over to the angora sitting on the exact center of the sofa like a polite and condescending duchess. "She's wonderful! You know, I'd like a cat like that myself. How long have you had her?"

Victor said nothing but Pauline told him a couple of weeks.

"Where'd you get her?"

"She came all by herself."

"Just wandered in, eh?" Julius stood close to the

cat, who took no notice of him. "Why didn't you come to me? I'd have been glad to have you."

"How could she have known that?" Pauline teased him, laughing. "You can't bear cats. Maybe she heard."

"But such a beauty!" Julius bent down and stroked the angora's back with his work-wise hands. Victor felt a sudden warm surge of affection for his hard-bitten friend. He was not callous after all. He could see animals, even a cat, as individuals: not just as man-ruled slaves.

White Lady measured Julius with a calm, distinguished surprise. Her face said: *You don't know me; I don't know you. No intimacies, please.* She stood up gracefully and crossed to the far corner of the sofa.

"A haughty creature." Faintly sheepish, Julius turned away. "Well, I can get along without her. We just won't be friends."

Again Victor saw Julius as a man to whom an animal was worthy of regard only when it served, fed, or flattered him. For a moment he wondered blankly how he had ever come to think of Julius as a friend.

Just then the angora stood up and leaped to the schoolmaster's breast. But her spring fell a little short and, abashed, she landed somewhere in the vicinity of his stomach.

"Come on," Victor said to her, suppressing his impulse to laugh. "Come on, climb! You have claws."

But she hung where she was, her bushy tail sweeping his knees in wide circles. Then she made another leap to his shoulder. She sat pressed close against Victor's neck and let her high purr be heard.

"I'm going," Julius said, "or I'll be jealous." He forced a laugh and waved his hat back at them over his shoulder.

Tasso already knew about the secret raids on Julius' rabbit warren. He himself did not touch a single rabbit, yet he watched loyally over Jibby while she fetched herself a tasty victim from the rabbit hutch. When he sensed danger coming he would grab Jibby between his teeth and carry her home.

Not once did Jibby resist—not even when it meant leaving the feast untasted. She accommodated herself to Tasso's decisions in complete trust. A-hunting she would go, and Tasso was her unfailing protector.

The twilight changed into night. Victor lit the big yellow hanging lamp in his study.

[147]

"Pauline!" he called. His wife came into the room. "Jibby is gone again."

"You don't believe it, Victor, but Jibby's just like all cats," she replied. "In the night they go out. Besides, I'll bet Tasso's with her right now."

"Funny, White Lady never goes roaming!"

"Perhaps she is exceptional, at that." Pauline was looking at the regal angora on the sofa. "However—"

Victor got up from his desk to cover Hansi's cage with a dark cloth. Off in the distance a dog howled. It sounded short and pained, the way a dog yelps when someone strikes him a heavy blow.

"What was that?"

"It sounded like over Julius' way," Pauline stammered.

"Tasso!" Victor cried, and Pauline stared at him with her hand over her mouth.

Julius had been on the warpath since dusk.

On the gentle rise of ground between the barn and the orchard sprawled his rabbit hutches. Just beyond, near the misshapen trunk of an old apple tree, Julius stood watch. A loaded rifle leaned against the trunk of the tree behind him, and in his hand he held a stout length of hickory.

It angered him that, even so, he did not see the

marauder arrive. A whisper and a scuffle inside the rabbit warren was the first he knew. Moving fast and light on his feet, he slipped inside, and there was Jibby feasting on her kill. Julius raised his club and brought it down across the cat's body. Jibby could not get away. Julius' kick sent her hurtling through the air. Just outside the inclosure, he caught her again and began stamping on her with his heavy boots.

At this juncture Tasso lunged in, and Julius gave him a heavy kick in the shoulder. The dog howled and stood back. A screen door slammed, and young Peter ran across the barnyard. He started toward the stunned cat on the ground. Over them the dog growled in his throat and got ready to spring at the man facing him with his stick raised above his head.

"Peter," snapped the farmer, "fetch mv rifle—in the orchard."

"No," cried the boy.

Tasso bared his fangs and fixed his eyes on Julius' throat.

The farmer knew Tasso's strength well and he was afraid. He fell back and lowered the stick to shield his face and neck. Seeing his chance, Tasso seized Jibby in his jaws and ran.

And thus, not long after Victor and Pauline had

heard him howl, Tasso appeared in the doorway, holding the mangled Jibby in his mouth. He laid her down on his mattress and looked up at his people in deep sorrow.

Jibby was a pitiful sight. Blood dripped from her nose and mouth. Her eyes were closed. Her mouth hung open without a sound and she gasped weakly for breath. Her chest might have been crushed. They thought she was dying.

"Kitty, kitty!" Shaken, Victor bent down over her but did not dare to touch her. The practical Pauline fetched a cold compress. She put it over Jibby, and at the touch the cat stirred.

"Who did this to you, Jibby?" Victor was beside himself with horror.

Julius, who had delayed only long enough to give his rebellious son a sound thrashing, came in like a conqueror. Pauline laid her free hand on Tasso.

"Well! I've caught it," Julius stormed. "Your cat, my friend! And your fine dog! They'll not be stealing rabbits again after the lesson I gave them."

"So?" Victor controlled himself with an effort.

"They'll remember me!" Julius was angry, talkative, and boastful. "And they'll remember their punishment."

"You call this punishment?" Victor said in an icy tone. "And who gave you the right to punish them?"

"What?" The farmer was thunderstruck. "What right have your animals to kill my rabbits?"

The schoolmaster stared at him without answering.

"So! You have nothing to say!"

Pauline straightened up beside the injured cat and gave Julius a little push.

"Go away," she said low and urgently. "Go away. He'll get angry and act like a devil."

"I'm not afraid," Julius shouted. "Right is on my side."

"How?" Victor demanded softly and stepped up close to the farmer. "What right? Why?"

Julius took a step back; but Victor's fist caught him in the face, and he rocked. Pressing his advantage, Victor grabbed Julius by the throat, pulled him forward again, and loosed a hail of blows on his astonished friend. Julius tried to hit back, but the schoolmaster's fists were drumming on his nose.

"Stop, Victor," he gasped. "Stop it!"

Victor did not stop. He kept on hammering at the farmer's nose until the blood ran freely and his hands were wet with it. Then he took Julius by the front of his jacket and flung him to the floor.

"Murder my friends, will you? On account of your slaughter-house rabbits." Without waiting for an answer he stood back, breathing hard, hands dropped at his sides. He was very pale.

Julius slowly got to his feet. He wiped the blood from his face with a handkerchief and asked softly: "Is she dead? Is your cat dead?"

"Not yet," Pauline said from beside Jibby. She had her back to the men and she had not moved. With her right hand, she eased the compress on Jibby's chest, and with her left she still held Tasso's paw against her own shoulder.

Suddenly the two men were calmer than a placid summer Sunday afternoon. Their voices were level.

"That's good," Julius said. "She'll live."

"Why didn't you ask me for damages instead of storming at my animals?" Victor asked.

"Damages?" Julius opened his eyes and mouth wide in astonishment. He had never thought of such a thing.

"Naturally. That was your right," Victor said reasonably.

Julius made his old gesture of bewilderment: he waved an arm.

"Would you have paid?" he said in real wonder.

"Of course." Victor felt magnanimous; he began to like Julius again. "That would have been your right. And we were friends and neighbors. But instead you behaved like an enemy."

"I'm not your enemy."

"No?" Victor began to pace the room, but his voice was still calm. "But look how disgracefully you manhandled the poor little thing. Look at her and tell me you are not an enemy."

Julius moved over to Jibby. He bent down beside Pauline in silence.

"I've been punished, Victor," he said after a moment. "Forgive me."

In the same reasonable tone he had been using before, Victor said: "When she walks around the room again, I'll forgive you. Not before."

Julius turned to Pauline.

"Do your best. Please." His eyes were hurt. The cat, they all felt without saying so, had become the symbol of their relationship.

"I'm no magician," Pauline answered him briefly.

Julius stood downcast as if waiting for something. Tasso had retreated into the kitchen. The angora had gone back to sleep. Quietly Julius let himself out the front door.

Pauline made a good sick bed for Jibby by the kitchen stove and poured a few drops of brandy into her mouth. The cold compresses soothed the wounds and the spirits seemed to arouse Jibby's life force. Eyes open, she lay staring straight before her. The bleeding had stopped, so it looked as if the internal injury was not serious. But still she was too weak to undertake the healing-method nature had given her: the endless licking of her tongue.

All night long Victor kept the compresses cool and moist; and the next day, while Victor was at the school, Pauline took up the nursing. By next evening Jibby was quite obviously going to live. She had no fever, and the milk they fed her with an eye dropper she swallowed greedily. After several days she lifted her head and drank by herself. The same night she began licking herself, her pink tongue snaking in and out and making an odd little gulping sound. Salved with her saliva, the wounds healed rapidly now; but she was still stiff and weak.

Victor stroked her lightly, and she accepted him though she gave no sign that the caress pleased her.

Every evening after the milking Julius came to the gate.

"How is she?" he asked.

For a while Pauline could only say: "Condition un-changed." But finally she told him: "A little better." On these sick calls the farmer made no move to come in. He heard the reports, nodded, and trudged away.

One day he entered the house; and Jibby, hearing his tread got up to flee, though she could barely move.

"That's a great advance, Julius," Pauline laughed. "A real improvement."

"Oh, my!" Julius scratched his head and gave a deep sigh.

In all the household, only the angora accepted Julius' advances. She even leaped upon his chest, quite frightening him the first time she did it. Then he stroked her clumsily while she perched on his shoulder. Her bright purring delighted him.

"This is beautiful! This is lovely!" Emboldened, he took a chance and crossed toward the desk where Victor bent over his work. "Don't be angry any more," he pleaded.

Victor looked up and resumed marking papers without a word.

"How long is this going to last?" Julius said, as if to himself.

Behind him in the kitchen door Pauline took pity on the lonely man.

"You know what Victor said," she reminded him, "and you know he always keeps his word. 'When the cat walks around the room again.' It won't be long now."

CHAPTER X

TASSO COMMITS MURDER

SUNDAY AFTERNOON a strange automobile stopped in front of the house. A moment or two later there was a gentle, uncertain knock at the door. Victor went to answer it. Before him stood a middle-aged, fashionably dressed woman with a little smile on her pretty face.

Before anyone could speak the white angora leaped

from the sofa and landed in the center of the study. The lady looked past the startled schoolmaster.

"So this is where you are, Mira!" she cried. "I thought so."

"Please come in," Victor said.

Their caller swept across the threshold. Mira paraded back and forth in front of the lady, her great plume of a tail making circles in the air. Her purr keyed higher into a sort of hum.

"I am Mrs. Lawber," the woman explained. "My husband is a lawyer in the city, but we live just about five miles from here—out along the mountain road, you know." She smiled brightly. "Perhaps you know my husband."

"I'm sorry," said Victor. He began to dislike the woman. Pauline came in from the back of the house, and he said: "This is my wife; Mrs. Lawber."

"But I know you," she said animatedly, ignoring Pauline and talking to Victor. Pauline spoke not a word. "I came directly to you," the lady went on. "I knew I'd find Mira here—a house that just loves animals," she gushed.

"Do you want to take Mira away?" Pauline asked.

"As if it were that simple!" Mrs. Lawber laughed. She was very gay. "Take her with me? You don't believe that yourself. People like you surely know— We don't own animals; they own us."

"Very true," Victor nodded, beginning to like her a little better.

"Really," she went on, "we're the dependent ones. They leave us without a will of our own and we're sacrificed to every mood they take on."

The false note in her voice struck Victor full force.

"But," he objected, "if you understand animals well, they have no moods."

Seated on the sofa, the lady drew herself up and glanced sideways at the angora nervously pacing the other half of the sofa beside her.

"Understand?" said the lady oratorically, as if she were addressing a courtroom. "When did I not understand you, Mira? Tell us yourself. When? We went away to a resort because the doctor prescribed a cure for me. Could I help that? Couldn't you have waited? Did the cook treat you badly?" Mrs. Lawber straightened her hat. "At any rate, I'm innocent. Why did you run away? And did you have to go so far?" She looked around the bare-floored study and stared a little when her gaze came around to the outlandish bird cage. "Is this place paradise?" Plainly she wanted Mira to answer no.

Pauline and Victor were silent, half amused, half annoyed.

"A bird in a cage!" she scolded. She turned to Jibby's sickbed, which only the day before they had moved in from the kitchen. "And you, poor little thing, you're not doing so well either, are you?"

"She is being nursed," Victor said curtly. "She was—"

"Oh, well, it's no business of mine," Mrs. Lawber cut him off.

Pauline ran out of patience.

"That's the first proper thing you've said since you came in," she began. "It's no business of yours. So how dare you make remarks about it?"

"I— I'm sorry," the lady visitor stammered. "Truly I am."

But Pauline was not appeased.

"Take your angora and get out of here," she said in exactly the polite tone another woman might employ urging someone to have a cup of tea.

"But— But—" The lady looked everywhere except at her hostess. "This is too much, really."

"I don't like high and mighty airs in my home," Pauline went on, crossing the room and standing quietly in front of the sofa.

"Come, Mira, let's go." Energetically Mrs. Lawber turned to the angora, picked her up, and held her tightly. "Mira!"

Mira had a different idea. She wriggled away from the lady and lay down in her corner of the sofa. Victor went up to her. His wife walked gracefully away and stood by the desk, watching the little tableau.

"Go, Mira," Victor said. "Go nicely. It's your mistress."

Mira jumped to Victor's shoulder, pressed herself against his neck and cheek, and pounded his back with her magnificent tail. She began a gay, high purr.

"What am I to do?" Victor was embarrassed.

"What you should do," Mrs. Lawber snapped, "is give her a good slap."

"I hit no animal." Trapped and flattered by the purring cat, he presented a droll sight in his helplessness. Pauline's shoulders shook with suppressed laughter. Mrs. Lawber stared a moment, and then she too had to laugh. Pauline joined her. The caller stood up, her gay self again.

"I've wasted time," she cried. "Keep the faithless vixen. Goodbye. It's been such a pleasure."

They heard the automobile drive off.

"I can't help feeling as if we'd stolen Mira," Victor said.

"I wish we had. What a woman!"

Mira stayed of her own plain will, and Victor and Pauline had nothing on their conscience. Yet Mira grew moody and unpredictable—pleasant one moment and hateful the next. And it was Tasso that suffered.

Now when Tasso came into the study, Mira pretended she did not know him and grew excited like any ordinary cat expecting to be attacked by a strange dog. She arched her back and spat wildly; but still the good Tasso went up to her and wagged his tail. Mira slapped out with a curved and nailed paw. Amiable Tasso took it as a game until the sharp claws tore his cheek open. He yowled and snapped at Mira's neck.

"Mira!" Victor intervened. "How can you insult your good friend?" He gathered her up and she nestled, soft as white velvet, in his arms. "Well," he said, "you're friends again."

The moody angora, however, continued to show her claws against Tasso day after day and again and again, until that peaceable citizen of the animal kingdom was outraged. His terrible jaws caught Mira's

back and swung her, loudly complaining, into the
air. There he shook her mercilessly and hurled her to
the floor. The beautiful Mira lay still.

Victor came in from the garden.

"What's biting you two?" he scolded.

Tasso wagged his half-curl of a tail eagerly. He was
ready for peace.

"Let them be," Pauline called from the kitchen.
"They're only playing."

"Funny kind of playing." Victor was examining his
dog. "Tasso's bleeding."

And indeed it was a serious affair. Lightning fast,
Mira pulled herself together and sprang at Tasso's
neck, mouth open, claws unsheathed and dangerously
curved. The bitter dog warded her off with a heavy
paw and then caught her by the breast and bit
hard. Mira sank down, blood gushing from her
chest.

"Tasso!" Victor shouted, grabbing the dog by the
shoulders and trying to pull him away. "Tasso!"

Pauline came running in.

Tasso did not hear. Tasso, the good, the gentle
Tasso, was no longer gentle, no longer good. He
meant to kill the malicious Mira. He would not let
her go. Raving, insensitive to the prods and threats

from his master, he sank his teeth deeper and deeper into Mira's snow-white breast. Her glistening coat was a bright mass of blood.

"He'll kill her!" Pauline cried out.

The otter hound's strength was greater than a man's. His jaws held the wounded angora tightly. Growling, he edged his muzzle along toward her windpipe. He found it and bit once again. The cat gasped, her throat rattled, and the dog still bit and growled. Even when he let go, he hovered over her, alert for any movement, ready to attack again and deliver a death blow.

Mira shuddered and lay still, her flanks oddly sunken.

Victor stood back. "How could a dog like Tasso commit murder?"

"He was irritated beyond endurance." Pauline had pulled Tasso to her and was stroking him. "You must realize that, Victor."

He stared at the dead cat and at Tasso, who had simply lain down where he was, gory nose on his paws—paws almost touching the thing he had killed. Victor was appalled—and not just by the fight: by this new revelation of the thin line between nature and domestication. He might have waked up and found a snake in bed with him. At last, helplessly, he said: "But Tasso!"

The dog, lying still and sad on the floor, pointed his ears at the sound of his name.

"Even the gentlest dog can become wild sometimes," Pauline said, moving to the window.

"He was always so patient," Victor protested.

"All patience has an end," Pauline said firmly, "or it wasn't patience." She gathered the dead Mira up in a cloth.

Victor went out into the yard and buried Mira, the grand lady, beside Rags, the jester. The mounds in the animal graveyard numbered six.

"She was so beautiful," he said when he came back indoors, hovering behind Pauline as she got their evening meal ready.

"What good is being beautiful?" Pauline, who was lovely herself, said over her shoulder. "No matter how beautiful anyone is—human being or cat—if she is also false, the devil will get into her in the end." She rattled the dishes.

"I'm too sentimental about animals," said Victor, who was thinking not of Mira but of his noble Tasso. "I preach taking them as they are and I am the first to forget it. I feel awfully silly." Tasso laid his paw on his master's arm. Victor looked into the dog's loving face. "That's good, Tasso; you're apologizing? We'll get on somehow, I guess."

Tasso did not stop wooing the teacher with his paw. "What else do you want of me?" Victor said sharply. But the dog's faithful gaze disarmed him. "Yes, Tasso, we're friends. It's all right."

What Tasso desired was not words but the hand of his beloved master. He waited. When Victor touched him gently on the head, he gave a loud bark between a sob and a cry of triumph. Beside himself with joy, the otter hound rushed crazily around the room, sounding his poignant bark and miraculously managing not to overturn everything in the kitchen. He headed back toward his master. Victor stood still and braced himself. The big dog hit his breast full tilt, almost knocking him over.

"Everything's all right, Tasso." Victor's spirits rose, for it was good to be friends again with his dog. He crossed Tasso's floppy ears over his nose. Taking one ear at a time, he wiped the rheum out of the corners of Tasso's eyes. It was a service greatly valued by the otter hound. "Now we'll have a feast of reconciliation," he added.

"Jibby's up," Pauline called from the next room,

where she was feeding the invalid. At the sound of her voice, Tasso rushed into the study, half-leaped upon her, and almost upset her. "Whoa, Tasso, whoa!" The otter hound, tongue panting happily, trotted back to the kitchen where Victor was putting some meat in his dish.

Jibby had indeed risen from her sickbed. She did not venture far; she sat close by her pallet, fearful, withdrawn into herself. Victor came in and patted her, but she behaved like an ill-humored, mistrustful stranger.

"Let her alone," Pauline advised. "She's just risen from the dead."

But Victor tried to take the cat in his arms. Jibby, however, pulled back in such a fiercely unfriendly way that it startled him.

"What's the matter with you, kitten? Aren't we friends any more? You're my friend, Jibby. Have you forgotten?"

But Jibby was not won over.

"What's the matter with her?" Victor turned to Pauline. "She's all right now, isn't she?"

Pauline looked at Jibby, then at Victor.

"I suppose it still hurts," she said. "So she should be left in peace." She stroked Jibby's back with a feather-touch. The cat cuddled close to her. She gave a brief, quiet purr. Pauline called out: "Hear that?"

"What?"

"She purred."

"Bravo!" said Victor, on his way to join Tasso in the kitchen. "I guess Jibby only wants her nurse," he told the otter hound.

Tasso left his dish and padded quietly into the study. Wagging his tail, he put a forepaw on the edge of Jibby's bed in greeting. The cat, squatting over on its farther side, arched her back and spat weakly. Tasso was surprised, but he made no move to force any intimacy. Jibby held her belligerent stance, back raised, moustache spread. Again she tried to spit at him, and Tasso beat a retreat.

"You see?" Pauline said, looking up at Victor and the dog standing together in the doorway. "She doesn't even recognize Tasso, and they were such good friends."

"What will come of this?"

"It will end all right. But it takes time. It can't happen over night. Right, kitten?"

The front door rattled. Tasso growled. Julius stuck his head in.

"How goes it, Pauline?" he asked, hopefully staring at Jibby's vacant sickbed.

"Better and better!" Pauline beamed.

Together Victor and his dog walked across the study to the desk.

"Well, and you?" Julius asked boldly enough, but his face looked worried. "Are you still angry?" The teacher sat down without a word or sign. "You know how sorry I am," Julius said. "You could at least talk." He scratched his head. "If I were an animal, you'd have been good to me a long time ago."

The truth of that hit home, but Victor still said nothing.

"Julius," Pauline answered instead, "you're a human being; and that makes a great difference. You're not innocent. You're responsible."

Tasso edged around between the farmer and his master, and growled threateningly.

"Everybody's against me here," Julius muttered.

"Nonsense," said Pauline, not looking up from Jibby.

"Nonsense? The dog growls at me. Does that mean he loves me?"

"Well, an animal like that doesn't forget what's

done to him. Tasso, I'm sure, remembers kindness and cruelty alike."

"Come here, Tasso," Julius coaxed. "Come on, I won't hurt you." He reached out a hand. But the dog snapped at the air between them and ducked away. Julius shook his head. "If Victor would talk to me, the dog wouldn't be sharp with me any more either."

At the words, all Victor's anger at Julius left him, but he said nothing; he felt he was being vindicated.

"You know the conditions Victor set up, Julius," Pauline was saying. "The cat must walk around the room again."

"Is she really getting better?" Julius stepped too close to where Jibby was lying. She jumped up with a spitting hiss, but she lurched weakly against Pauline's knees when she tried to run.

"There's your answer, Julius," said Pauline, picking Jibby up and holding her tight.

CHAPTER XI

JIBBY THE CAT

NO TWO WAYS about it, Jibby was well.

She got back her old spirits. Thin but happy she paraded around the room, carrying her tail high. When Victor took her up in his arms, she cuddled securely on his chest and purred like a spinning top. He loved it when she mounted his shoulder, rubbed her head under his chin, and met his tenderness with tenderness of her own.

Jibby's new-found vitality took her all over the house. Joyfully wagging his tail, Tasso escorted her and watched over her steps.

"Well! That's better," crowed Julius from the front door, rubbing his hands together happily.

Tasso retreated to his corner and growled. Jibby stiffened and leaped on the chair arm by Pauline. Julius stood still just inside the door. After a moment Jibby jumped down and took up her romp with Tasso.

"Well?" grinned the farmer. "Does that count?"

Victor laughed and stood up.

"It counts!" Pauline cried.

"Well, then— Do you talk to me again?" Julius held out a hand to his friend and Victor took it firmly. "We've had a bad time," Julius said, smiling a little.

The sun poured its warmth over the garden, the house, and the fields. The busy doves walked around outside, heady with love. In the window hung Hansi's out-sized cage. The yellow bird trilled the long, melodic bars of his composition for a flute. On a sunny square of the spacious study floor lay Jibby the cat, pleasantly stretched out. Tasso watched over her tenderly. Victor sat quietly working at his desk while Pauline went about her household chores, lightly treading between her kitchen and the big room.

It was a nice peaceful day.

A magpie fluttered in, cackled a little, and flew about acting as if he were an old crony of theirs and had lived there always. Jibby lifted her head, stared with curiosity yet without surprise at the new guest, and lay back down in comfort. Tasso walked amiably over to the magpie and wagged his tail.

Head stretched forward, the magpie tripped over to Jibby and pecked gently at her with his big bill. Jibby waved her paws at him lazily, and the magpie bent back and let out a deep call that sounded like "Oha!" At once he was back again at Jibby's side. He poked his bill into her flank.

Jibby went into action. But the magpie flew around the room and perched at last high on the hanging lamp.

"Oha!" he cried in deep, full tones, looking around with wise eyes.

Side by side Tasso and Jibby stood on the floor below, looking up at the swaying lamp. The magpie cackled as if it were laughing, suddenly flew down to the floor, and dived for Jibby. Tasso placed himself in front of the cat he had elected to protect. Nothing happened, for the magpie turned playful and the two animals showed they halfway understood it was a game. But, still a little distrustful, they kept a sharp lookout.

In a surprise maneuver the magpie landed square

upon Tasso's back and began to poke around in the dog's neck. Tasso shook himself violently. The bird lost his footing. He fluttered toward the floor, but he promptly lifted himself up again when he saw Jibby lying ready to welcome him with outstretched paws.

With an incessant whir and flutter and flap, the magpie lifted, sank down, and flew up again, never quite settling on the floor. It was like teasing. Tasso lifted and lowered his head, while Jibby pounced here and there in vain attempts to catch the bird. Then the magpie flew back to his perch on the hanging lamp.

"Oha!" he chortled.

"That bird will come to a bad end," Pauline predicted.

"They're really playing this time." Victor gave a happy sigh.

The whole house was in an uproar, and it was only when Julius arrived that the situation became critical. The magpie absolutely would not stand for his being in the room. He flew straight at the farmer in a frontal attack. Julius took it as a joke.

"You certainly have unusual animals in this house," he laughed.

"Isn't he beautiful?" smiled Pauline.

"Beautiful," Julius pronounced agreeably. "If it would leave me in peace."

The magpie, wings flapping fast, kept pushing against the man. When Julius slapped at the magpie with his cap, the bird dodged the blow cleverly, fluttered to his shoulder, and pecked his cheek.

"That hurts!" exclaimed Julius, forcing a laugh. Again he aimed a blow with his cap. "Victor! Call off your little vulture!"

"It doesn't mind me." Victor was laughing hard. "Besides, it's not a vulture; it's a magpie."

Julius turned his head here and there.

"Oha!" shrieked the magpie into his ear, all at once in full voice. Julius flinched painfully.

"Help me, Victor!"

But everybody was helpless with so much laughing.

Perhaps the rasp in Julius' voice scared the magpie; he fluttered and poked twice as hard as before.

"Well!" Julius grunted. "It's come to this. A bird throws me out!" He ducked through the door and closed it quickly behind him.

Pauline and Victor sat holding their sides and gasping for breath. Jibby, forgetting the magpie, climbed up beside the teacher.

"So, my kitten," he welcomed her. She climbed on

delicate feet to his shoulder, pushed her head under his chin, and purred. But she did not stay long. Down she jumped and streaked away from him. She slipped out the door.

"Where away, Jibby? Where are you off to in such a hurry?" Sober now, Victor stepped out in front of the cottage to call her back. He was just in time to see her tail disappear behind the small ridge that marked the edge of the field across the way.

"Let her go," Pauline said. "She's off on a mouse-hunt."

"She always runs out on the road," Victor worried. "Send Tasso."

"Tasso!" The dog wagged his tail and pointed his ears attentively. "Fetch the kitten, Tasso!"

Long after dark the dog came back with the cat dangling from his jaws. Jibby jumped up from the floor where he deposited her, and sat on the sofa washing herself.

"Out on the road again," Victor scolded her.

"The trouble with you, Victor," said Pauline, "is you don't know cats."

"Oh," said the teacher. Again he'd been caught trying to convert Jibby, the cat. For wasn't it in her nature to wander the open road alone one day—and charm a man the next?

"Tasso's laughing!" said Pauline.

They turned together and looked at Tasso. His mouth open in something that was neither a bark nor a yawn. The amber eyebrows worked up and down quizzically and the corners of his mouth stretched in a wide grin.

"Now what on earth is Tasso laughing about?" said the schoolmaster.